MIND READER

'Mind Reader *is great*' – **Literacy and Learning**

My favourite of your books is Mind Reader *because it makes you want to read on. I was glued to it*'
– Boy, 13, Northern Ireland

'*I have just finished* Mind Reader *and it is one of the best books I've ever read. I really liked the way Matt seems to be talking to the reader. I had to keep reading the book to see what would happen next*'
– Girl, 10, Northants

Pete Johnson says, 'The inspiration for this story is my deep curiosity … all right, nosiness … about other people. How I'd love to know what my family and friends are thinking. But I wouldn't only use my crystal on people I knew … no one would be safe from me. The very hardest thing would be keeping my amazing power a secret. I'd just have to tell someone!'

Pete Johnson has been a film extra, a film critic for Radio One, an English teacher and a journalist. However, his dream was always to be a writer. At the age of ten he wrote a fan letter to Dodie Smith, author of *The Hundred and One Dalmatians*, and together they communicated for many years, Dodie Smith was the first person to encourage him to be a writer.

He has written many books for children as well as plays for the theatre and Radio 4, and is a popular visitor to schools and libraries.

Some other books by Pete Johnson

THE PROTECTORS
TEN HOURS TO LIVE

For younger readers

BUG BROTHER
PIRATE BROTHER

MIND READER DOUBLE

PETE JOHNSON

PUFFIN BOOKS

PUFFIN BOOKS

Published by the Penguin Group
Penguin Books Ltd, 80 Strand, London WC2R 0RL, England
Penguin Putnam Inc., 375 Hudson Street, New York, New York 10014, USA
Penguin Books Australia Ltd, 250 Camberwell Road, Camberwell, Victoria 3124, Australia
Penguin Books Canada Ltd, 10 Alcorn Avenue, Toronto, Ontario, Canada M4V 3B2
Penguin Books India (P) Ltd, 11 Community Centre, Panchsheel Park, New Delhi – 110 017, India
Penguin Books (NZ) Ltd, Cnr Rosedale and Airborne Roads, Albany, Auckland, New Zealand
Penguin Books (South Africa) (Pty) Ltd, 24 Sturdee Avenue, Rosebank 2196, South Africa

Penguin Books Ltd, Registered Offices: 80 Strand, London WC2R 0RL, England

www.penguin.com

Mind Reader first published 1998
Mind Reader: Blackmail first published 1999
Published in this edition 2003
1

Text copyright © Pete Johnson, 1998, 1999
All rights reserved

The moral right of the author has been asserted

Set in Bembo

Made and printed in England by Clays Ltd, St Ives plc

British Library Cataloguing in Publication Data
A CIP catalogue record for this book is available from the British Library

ISBN 0–141–31308–0

Contents

MINDREADER

Contents

Chapter One
The Dangerous Gift

FIRST OF ALL don't be scared of me. By myself I have no special powers at all.

My name is Matt, nickname Spud because my nose looks a bit like a potato.

I'm the most ordinary boy you'll

ever meet. Or I was until . . . now I'm jumping ahead. And I want to tell you everything, just as it happened.

It all started when I was left something in Mrs Jameson's will. I was totally amazed. I'd never been left anything in a will before.

Mrs Jameson was a very old lady. I first visited her with a harvest festival gift from our school.

She frowned at me. "None of it looks very fresh – and bananas give me indigestion, you know."

"Oh, sorry about that," I replied, not sure what else to say.

"Still, I suppose I could eat some of it. You'd better come in."

We sat in her kitchen. She poured me a glass of orange juice. Then I asked her if she liked living on her own.

"Yes of course I like it," she snapped. "Other people cause problems. You can't trust one of them." She glared at me. I hastily changed the subject.

Around her neck she was wearing a crystal. It caught my eye right away. She saw me looking at it.

"This crystal was left to me by my great aunt who took a shine to me. A strange woman; used to call herself a wizard. You didn't know there were any female wizards, did you?"

"No," I said. Actually I didn't know many male wizards either — not personally anyway.

She leaned forward. "This crystal is priceless. But no one else knows my crystal's true worth – and that's how it must stay. Otherwise I'd never have a moment's peace."

She was exaggerating now. She must be.

Still, I must admit the crystal fascinated me. Maybe because there were flashes of so many colours in it.

"I love all the colours you can see," I said, "especially that sky blue at the centre." Then I added hastily: "It is blue, isn't it?"

She looked puzzled by my question so I thought I'd better explain. "Only I'm what they call colour-deficient. I can see every single colour, I just see it in different ways. So I might see red as brown and brown as red. Blue and purple are pretty confusing too. That's why I asked."

"The crystal is blue in the centre, just as you said," she interrupted. Her eyes were blue too, and they were staring intently at me.

"Oh good, because sometimes I can make embarrassing mistakes. I went into a pet shop once and asked for the gold hamster."

For the first time she gave a wheezy laugh, then said slowly, "You just see in your own world of colour, that's all. I expect my crystal is more beautiful through your eyes than anyone else's." I really liked the way she said that. She made me feel special.

After that I visited her almost every day. We sat in her kitchen talking about practically everything. But then she became ill. She had pneumonia. She didn't want to leave her home but the doctor insisted. She'd only been in hospital for a couple of days when she died quite suddenly. She'd done that just to spite the doctor. That's what I told myself to try and cheer myself up.

I thought about her a lot over the next few days.

Then I discovered she'd left her precious crystal to me. She'd written me a letter too. On the envelope she'd put: "STRICTLY PRIVATE: FOR MATTHEW COLLINS ONLY." I'm not sure exactly why, but my hands shook as I opened the envelope.

Inside was her letter to me. Her handwriting was very shaky and difficult to read. Finally I made out: "Dear Matthew, I am leaving you my most valuable possession in gratitude for all those enjoyable hours we spent talking together. I do not want anyone else to discover how special my crystal is – ONLY YOU. But Matthew, you must keep the secret and you must be careful, because my gift can be VERY DANGEROUS as you will discover . . ."

This was followed by some squiggles which I couldn't read. The letter wasn't finished.

I stared and stared at it. What did Mrs Jameson mean about my crystal being very dangerous? That didn't make any sense. And what would I discover?

Then my mum peeked over my shoulder at the letter. "Poor thing," she said, "she was probably wandering in her mind when she wrote that. I expect she just wanted to make sure you took care of her gift."

But I didn't think that was true. Mrs Jameson's mind was sharp right to the end. She was trying to tell me something about the crystal, something very important.

But what?

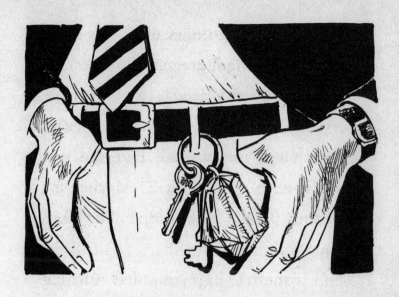

Chapter Two
Secrets of the Crystal

I PUT THE crystal on a keyring. I wore it to school on a loop on my belt. Even some of the teachers admired it.

After school the crystal sat on the telly in my bedroom. When the sun came down the crystal would shine all

these different colours on to my wall:
blue, pinkish red, green, yellow.

Then it did seem like a magic
crystal. I thought of Mrs Jameson's
great aunt, the wizard. Did she cast
spells with this crystal? Maybe she
turned people she didn't like into
slugs.

I wouldn't have minded turning
Craig Atkins into a slug. He was a
new boy at our school who just
loved himself. He was always boasting
about his house and how he had a
heated swimming pool and a pool table
and . . . but I never listened to him.

I hated him. I especially hated the
way he smiled – like a cat who's not
only swallowed all his cream but all
yours too.

Then, just messing about, I picked up my crystal and said, "Hocus pocus, make Craig Atkins into a slug."

I was only fooling around and really didn't expect anything to happen.

But something did.

The crystal started getting warmer. It was like when you put your hand on a radiator which has just been switched on. You can feel the heat stealing up your fingers, can't you?

Well, it was the same with my crystal. And then the crystal went on getting hotter, until in the end it seemed to be burning into my hands. I wasn't able to hold it any more. I let it drop on to my bed.

For a few seconds my fingers were still tingling. I couldn't believe how hot that crystal had become. I shivered with the shock.

I gave the crystal a quick prod. It was cold again. Yet as soon as I picked it up exactly the same thing happened: the crystal got warm, then after thirty-four seconds (I timed it) it became so hot I had to let it go.

But how weird.

I was tempted to run downstairs and tell Mum and Dad. But Alison, my older sister and my mortal enemy, was also downstairs and I didn't want her knowing about this. She'd already cast envious eyes on my crystal, saying how it was wasted on me.

And some words from Mrs Jameson's note rushed into my head: "You must keep the secret."

I'd never heard of a crystal which could get hot all by itself. That would certainly make it very valuable.

But Mrs Jameson hadn't just written "valuable". She'd put "very dangerous" as well.

I still didn't understand that. Then I suddenly thought: what if the crystal can put spells on people too? What if one second Craig is posing about by his pool and the next he's scuttling about as a slug.

I'd love to see his parents' faces when this slug starts chattering to them, claiming to be their marvellous son.

Of course I was only fooling about. Craig would be back at school tomorrow, wouldn't he?

Chapter Three
A Tremendous Discovery

FIRST OF ALL Craig wasn't at school. My hopes began to rise. I'd become quite keen on him turning into a slug.

But at breaktime there he was: an annoying grin plastered all over his face as usual. He was wearing his new designer-label green shirt; he looked like a long, processed pea in it. To make matters worse he was talking to Cally.

Despite what you may have heard, Cally is not exactly my girlfriend. She is more a mate. My best mate, to be exact.

Maybe you think that's a bit unusual. But she's been my best mate for more than two years now; since not long after she moved here, in fact. At first I'd see her at school and out walking Bess, her pet spaniel, but I never really spoke to her until the day Bess ran off. And I was the one who found her.

Cally was so relieved. Her parents were too – they invited me in for tea. I felt shy. I wasn't sure what to say. I noticed Cally was watching football on the telly so I said, "Oh, you like football, then, do you?"

"Thought I'd only like netball, did you?" she replied with heavy sarcasm. "Whenever a girl shows an interest in football why do all boys' chins hit the ground?"

"My chin's just fine," I replied. "I bet you know far more about football than me, anyway."

She did. Much more. But then she'd gone to her first football match – with her dad – when she was only four. At five she became her team's mascot.

"Who is your team now?" I asked.

"Spurs, of course," she smiled. "They're the only team worth supporting." She told me all about

Spurs, showed me her Spurs calendar, her Spurs torch, her four Spurs shirts.

She made it all sound quite exciting. That's when I thought I might as well support Spurs too. I'm still not such a mad fan as Cally, but I come quite close these days.

Her dad would sometimes take us to major Spurs games. It's so much better than watching it on the telly, for when you're there you're a part of it. Her dad was hoping to get tickets for the big Spurs versus Arsenal match. I was really looking forward to that.

Anyway, Cally and I go round together a lot and we get on really well. In fact, there's only one subject we disagree strongly about: Craig Atkins.

If Cally thought that he was an utter turnip-head – and she said she did – why was she always talking to him? Like now. I had a horrible feeling she was more impressed by him than she was letting on.

That's why I decided to tell her about my crystal. After all, my crystal was much more exciting than anything Craig could boast about. In fact, my crystal was probably the only one of its kind in the world.

I planned to tell Cally at lunchtime.

I stood waiting for her in the corner of the playground where we usually meet up.

I wanted to check the crystal was still working. I held it and nothing seemed to be happening. My heart sank. Maybe it only worked at night. Out of the corner of my eye I saw Craig walking towards me. He was the last person I wanted to talk to now. I deliberately looked away.

Then heat started to surge through again. I let out a great sigh of relief. In the back of my head I could hear Mrs Jameson whisper: "You must keep the secret." I felt a stab of guilt. But I would swear Cally to secrecy and I wouldn't tell anyone else. Not ever.

Then I heard another voice whisper: "Great that Cally's dad has got some tickets for the Spurs versus Arsenal match! I bet she takes me not Spud this time. He's so boring."

I recognized the voice instantly. It was Craig. I jumped around, thinking he was right behind me, that was how close he sounded. But in fact he was still a couple of metres away from me.

I let go of the crystal.

He grinned at me. "Waiting for Cally, are you?" He said this so casually I could only stutter, "Yes." Then he gave me this big, friendly wave and he was gone.

I stared after him. I couldn't believe the way he'd blurted all that out to me then acted so cool. He must be very sure of himself.

And why had Cally told him about her dad having the tickets rather than me?

I was very uneasy. And for the moment I forgot all about my crystal.

I let Cally know what Craig had

said. She was totally amazed. "I just happened to mention to him that my dad had got the tickets, that's all. I was going to tell you too."

"Were you?"

"Of course I was," she laughed. "I only told him because he was showing off as usual and I wanted to shut him up."

"I see." I laughed as well, half-reassured.

After school we confronted Craig together. He played a blinder. He denied saying anything to me about Cally's football tickets. He claimed they were the last thing on his mind.

He gave quite a performance. I must admit that. He even swore on his life that he hadn't said anything to me.

Still, he could deny it as often as he liked. I'd heard him.

On the way home (Cally's house is on the way to mine) I said to her, "Craig's trying to cover up now by pretending he didn't say anything about your tickets. Still, you know Craig, his face would explode if he told the truth."

Cally laughed and nodded in agreement. She said, "Everyone's been asking me about the Spurs–Arsenal match. My dad was so lucky to get tickets. People keep coming up to me saying what big Spurs fans they are, and can they come with me."

I stiffened.

"Perhaps", she went on, "I should put all their names into a hat, or maybe

I should have a quiz about Spurs and let the biggest fan come. What do you think?"

I was too hurt to reply. What was she playing at? I was her best mate, therefore I should go with her. End of story. I decided having these tickets had really gone to her head.

Well, I'd show her I didn't care. I still had my amazing crystal. Cally was going to get a shock in a moment.

But it wasn't her who got the shock – it was me.

For I suddenly heard her whisper: "Craig sounded as if he was telling the truth. Did Matt make all that up about the tickets just to turn me against Craig? I don't like that."

I was stunned, not just by what Cally

was saying but the way she was speaking, as if I wasn't there. Was she trying to be funny?

I turned to argue with her. She was still babbling away about how I didn't own her but her lips weren't moving.

HER LIPS WEREN'T MOVING.

In fact, her whole face was completely still.

What was going on here?

The hairs rose along the back of my head.

This was so weird. It was as if Cally's voice had somehow escaped from her body. And I could hear it so clearly. It sounded as if she was whispering something very confidentially in my ear.

Only she wasn't.

Really, she was deep in thought, completely unaware that I could hear her.

The crystal was becoming very hot now. I had to let it go. At once Cally's voice sprang back into her body again.

I gaped at her in amazement. My heart was beating furiously.

"What's the matter?" asked Cally. This time her lips were moving again.

"The matter?" I stuttered.

"You look like you've just seen a ghost . . . Are you all right?"

"No, I feel a bit sick, that's all." And actually my stomach was like jelly. "So I won't stop off at your house this evening, I'll go straight back."

"Yeah, sure. But will you be all right?"

I nodded. "Say hello to Bess for me – and Craig really did say all that stuff, you know. You've got to believe me."

"Don't be silly. Of course I believe you," said Cally.

I stumbled off.

"Matt."

I turned round. Cally gave me a little smile. "No, I'll tell you later," she said.

I walked a few metres, but my legs felt like lead. Then I stopped. What had just happened didn't make any sense. People only spoke without moving their lips in films that hadn't been dubbed properly.

Either I was going mad or I had just made the most tremendous discovery about my crystal.

Chapter Four
Testing the Crystal

I STARED DOWN at the crystal. I hardly dared breathe on it.

Now I know what Mrs Jameson meant: it was priceless. For this crystal would let me peer into people's minds. I could discover the most top-secret information.

Actually, I already had.

Craig didn't say a word about the Spurs tickets. He only thought it and I "overheard" him. No wonder he was so indignant.

Still, it served him right for even thinking it. And at least I knew what Craig was up to.

"I have the power to read minds." I kept muttering this over and over to myself, just as if I were casting a spell.

I still couldn't take it in.

I had to test out the crystal again. This time I decided to try it on a complete stranger.

But who?

People were walking past so quickly and I couldn't start trailing after one of them. They'd get suspicious. Then I stopped at the sweet shop. The couple who owned the shop were away. I didn't know the woman who was standing in for them.

I went inside the shop.

"Hello," I said, smiling cheerily at the woman.

She just gave me a frosty glare in reply.

I told her what I wanted, then I pointed my crystal towards her. The crystal grew warmer. She was weighing up my sweets. She didn't look up. But all at once I overheard: "Shall I wear my blue hat or my red one to the wedding? The blue hat matches my jacket but the red one is more expensive."

She handed me the sweets. I gave her the exact money, then said, gravely, "I should wear the blue hat if I were you." She looked so shocked I thought her head was going to start spinning.

"How do you know that?" she gasped at last.

"Don't worry, I know everything," I replied. "Do enjoy your wedding, won't you. Goodbye for now."

She didn't answer, just put out a hand as if to stop herself from falling.

Outside the shop I laughed and laughed. The look on her face – I'll never forget that.

What a brilliant crack! It was only afterwards I wondered if I'd been a bit . . . well, reckless. For I'd drawn attention to myself. That woman could tell her friends. Gossip could start.

I decided I had to be more careful, more discreet.

For if anyone ever found out about my crystal . . . well, the world would be at my door, wouldn't it? I'd never have a moment's peace. I certainly would never dare wear my crystal in case someone tried to steal it. I'd probably have to keep it in a vault.

Plus if the government ever found out about it, they'd want to perform tests on it.

And only one person was going to do tests on this crystal – me.

Chapter Five
Talking to the Dead

NEXT DAY I bought a notebook so that I could jot down everything I discovered about my crystal. Only I decided it was too risky to refer to the crystal directly, especially if my notebook got into the wrong hands (for example, my sister's).

So I gave my crystal a code name. I called it "The Third Ear".

And then I jotted down all I'd discovered about my "third ear". Some amazing things, actually.

For instance, if I wanted to know what someone was thinking I just pointed my crystal in their direction. And it didn't matter how far away they were.

I discovered that when I was playing football. I'm not really good at football. I just like playing it, even if I usually end up in goal. I was in goal, that day. We were playing Wycliffe, the school down the road from us and our big rivals.

I let in two goals but also made a

couple of pretty good saves. So it was two-all when right at the end of the match came a penalty.

Talk about pressure: everyone was calling out things to me. But I was only listening to one person. (The crystal was tucked safely in my pocket.) He was a few metres away from me. But when I tipped the crystal towards him I picked up: "I'll let their goalie think I'm going for the left corner and then do the opposite."

Of course I dived to the right and made the most magnificent save, even if I say so myself. My team went crazy. Someone even called me the supreme penalty saver.

And I just lapped it up.

Now what else could my crystal do?

Well, it travelled through glass. I could stand by the kitchen window and pick up what my mum was thinking in the garden (very boring it was too). But it couldn't travel through walls (tried this a couple of times) and it didn't work on the telephone or with the television.

What about with animals? It would be great if the crystal was able to pick up their thoughts. I decided to test it out on the cleverest dog I know – Bess. She's incredibly obedient. It's no wonder she's won so many prizes and looks certain to win lots more.

My moment came after school. I was round Cally's house. She went inside to get us some drinks. I was left in the garden with Bess. I called her over. She came at once.

And when she saw the crystal she pricked up her ears and seemed really excited. But all I picked up was this strange, whooshing noise, just like when you hold a shell up to your ear.

Later when Bess was asleep she started whining and shaking her legs. She was dreaming. I've always wanted to know what dogs dream about. I nudged the crystal towards her but all I got was that whooshing noise again.

It seemed the crystal only worked on humans. Then I had a crazy thought: might the crystal work on dead bodies as well as live ones?

I'd always wanted to know if we could contact the dead.

Maybe I was about to find out. I

might discover what happens after you die.

Shudders ran through me.

This was getting creepy – but fascinating.

I decided to test out my theory at the local cemetery. I went there in the early evening. I wanted it to be dark – but not too dark. I slumped down by a grave. My hand was shaking. The crystal started to get warm, then this croaky old voice began whispering in my ear.

"Are you all right?" he asked.

"I'm fine," I spluttered. "How about you?" Then I realized that was a stupid question, for if he was all right he wouldn't be where he was.

"I mean, what's it like . . . there?"

"What's it like?" he repeated. That's when I realized that not only could I hear a dead man – I could feel his breath on my ear.

I whirled round and nearly cannoned into this old man. We stood gaping at each other.

"Are you sure you're all right, lad?" he quavered, at last.

Very embarrassed now, I stuttered, "Oh yes. It's just I thought you were someone else. Bye."

I ran all the way home.

Later I wondered if I should repeat the experiment. But I wasn't eager to return to that graveyard. Not on my own, anyway. Instead, I decided to test my crystal on one of the living dead – Mr Rickets, the history teacher!

Chapter Six
Amazing, Sensational News

EVERYONE MESSES ABOUT in Mr
Rickets' class. It's sort of compulsory.

We used to have these great ink
fights in his class. I'd go home with my
shirt absolutely covered. Trust parents
to ruin the fun by complaining. Now

teachers – and sometimes the headmaster – patrol around outside Mr Rickets' class. They pretend they're not but at the slightest sign of any trouble one of them always pops in.

Mr Rickets was talking about Henry VIII that day, I think. I couldn't be sure as everything he says goes through my head and falls out on the other side.

I directed the crystal towards him and tuned in. This really whiny voice came through, moaning about how he could never engage this class's interest even though he had tried so hard. Now all he had to look forward to was his cup of coffee at breaktime.

It was quite sad really. The crystal was becoming hot and I was about to tune out when I heard: "So tired and my wig's so itchy again."

His wig?

Hold the front page! Rickets wears a wig.

This was amazing, sensational news. For while we had often commented on the awfulness of Rickets' hair – it was all permed and feathery – no one had guessed that it wasn't his own.

I was so excited I whispered the news to Cally at once. Of course I couldn't say I'd "overheard" Rickets, so instead I claimed I'd seen the join at the back of his head.

That news went round our classroom like wildfire. Soon everyone was studying Rickets with more attention than they'd ever given him before. Rickets even gave us a small smile. He must have thought he'd suddenly become interesting.

He set us some work. We all piled up to his desk to ask him stupid questions, while scrutinizing the back of his head. Then Andy Grey gave me the thumbs up – he'd spotted the join too.

I'd been proved right. Pleased by my discovery, I was eager to find out more about the wig. So at the end of the lesson I stood asking Mr Rickets about homework, while activating my crystal. I didn't pick up anything more about the wig – but I discovered there was going to be a surprise test on Henry VIII tomorrow.

Usually Rickets' surprise tests caught me out. But not this time.

On the way home I tuned into Cally. She still hadn't offered me the other ticket for the Spurs versus Arsenal match. I was anxious because of Craig. He was still hanging around with Cally. Today I had heard him boasting to her about all his computer games and CDs. Was he impressing her?

But she wasn't thinking about Craig. She was worrying about her school work. Her parents thought she should be getting higher marks. They'd been nagging her about that. And she really didn't want to let her parents down. But she was doing her best. Why couldn't they see that?

I felt very sorry for Cally. That's why I blurted out: "I've got a feeling there might be a test on Henry VIII tomorrow."

She looked puzzled. "Rickets never said anything."

"Oh, you know how he loves to give us surprise tests. There'll be a test tomorrow. You'll see."

Sure enough, next day there was a test on Henry VIII. By the following lesson Rickets had marked the test, and guess who got top marks . . . Well, in fact Cally did. She got three more marks than me. I came second. But that was cool because Cally was so happy.

The day was spoilt though by someone (I'm sure it was Craig) scrawling on the board: RICKETS WEARS A WIG. Underneath he'd drawn this cartoon of a bald man. (A two-year-old could have drawn something better.)

And Rickets saw it. We expected him to explode, put the whole class in detention. Instead, he just picked up the board rubber and erased the offending picture.

He didn't say a word. But his eyes seemed to have closed up. And I knew – without needing to consult the crystal – that he was feeling sick inside.

He had massive problems keeping classes in order anyway. Now, thanks to me, he had a fresh one – because of course the whole school knew about his wig by now.

I felt more than a bit sick too. I'm

sure I wasn't using the crystal as Mrs Jameson intended. I was acting just like a pickpocket, foraging around in people's heads and stealing their secrets. You've heard of peeping Toms. I was the first listening Tom.

But later I changed my mind. After all, if I had supersonic hearing you wouldn't expect me to plug up my ears every time I went out, would you?

So what's the difference with my crystal?

I did make this pledge, though. Everything I found out by 'tuning-in' would remain in confidence, save for anything which might do me or my friends harm.

That was fair, wasn't it?

From now on I was determined to

use my crystal properly and not make any more mistakes.

But I did – an even worse one too.

Chapter Seven
End Of a Friendship

ON SATURDAY MORNING I went to the
Spring Fair at our school with Cally. I
had to lend her five pounds as her
parents never give her much pocket
money, but I didn't mind. Craig was
prowling around there too.

On one of the stalls was the biggest jar of sweets I'd ever seen. It was enormous. You could win all those sweets if you guessed how many were in the jar. People kept asking the man in charge of the stall to give them a clue. Every time he smiled but refused. Then Craig announced he knew how many sweets were in the jar.

If Craig won the sweets he'd go on about it for weeks . . . centuries. It would be yet another trophy for him to show off to Cally about.

I had no choice but to enter the competition too. Luckily my crystal had "overheard" the organizer. I knew exactly how many sweets were in the jar.

And so I won it.

I strolled triumphantly around the fair with my jar of sweets – remarkably heavy it was too. A little voice inside my head wondered if I'd cheated. But I swept the voice away by pointing out that if I hadn't butted in Craig would have certainly won, as his guess was the nearest after mine. So actually I'd saved the world from a very tragic event.

Also, I shared my sweets around which was more than Craig would have done.

Cally was dead impressed. "But you guessed it exactly right. How did you do that?"

"I'm a genius."

She laughed.

"And I had inside information."

She laughed again.

"No, I was just lucky, I suppose," I said finally.

"You've been very lucky recently, haven't you?" said Cally. "And perhaps you'll go on being lucky," she added, with a teasing smile. She wouldn't say any more. But I took that to mean she was going to let me have the other Spurs ticket.

And about time too. I was her best friend and I had helped her get top marks in the History test. I deserved that ticket.

But on Monday I received a big shock. I was sitting in a lesson, with the jar of sweets beside me. I still had hundreds left. And I was just casually tuning into a few people, or surfing as

I call it. It wasn't very exciting — most of them were just thinking about food — but then I directed my crystal at Craig.

To be honest, I didn't enjoy tuning into him. I hated to hear his voice whispering in my ear. Yuk! But I had to know what the enemy was thinking.

Craig must have noticed me glancing at him because I "overheard": "I'd love to tell Spud, but Cally's sworn me to secrecy. Shame. Because if he knew Cally was coming round my house tonight . . ." Then he started to laugh in his head. Horrible braying sounds which instantly gave me a migraine.

All day I walked around in a fog of misery. I didn't get a chance to say anything to Cally until we were walking home together.

I told myself to be calm, be cunning. So I asked as lightly as I could manage: "What are you doing this evening, then?"

Cally shrugged her shoulders. "Nothing much, just do my homework and wash my hair, the usual." Then she changed the subject.

Of course I knew she was lying. It was becoming harder to control my anger. "I see Craig's still creeping around you just so you'll give him the Spurs ticket."

Cally's face reddened.

"He's got a nerve, hasn't he, trying to steal my ticket?" I went on.

"Your ticket!" she exclaimed.

"Yes, you're going to give the other ticket to me, aren't you?"

Cally didn't say anything, just gave a strange kind of half-laugh. Was she amused? Was she starting to feel guilty?

My crystal would know.

This is what it picked up . . . "Just sick of Matt going on about this Spurs ticket all the time like it's his property. Well, I'll show him. When I go round to Craig's house tonight, I'll see if he wants the ticket."

I snatched my hand away from the crystal. I felt as if I'd just been punched in the stomach. I hardly spoke to Cally after that – and she hardly spoke to me either.

All evening my head was in a whirl. I wanted to go to Craig's house –

sorry, mansion — and smash all his windows. I wanted to do something bold and dramatic and nasty. I plotted all sorts of impossible things in my head.

I hardly slept that night.

Next morning I arrived at school to see Cally and Craig laughing together in the playground. Something in me just snapped. I stormed over to Cally. "I hope you and Craig enjoy the football match together," I sneered. "And I want the five pounds I lent you on Saturday. I'm always lending you money and not getting it back." I was practically shouting now. People were gathering round. But before Cally could reply I'd shot away again.

She didn't sit with me in

registration. Well, I didn't care. But at breaktime she was waiting for me by my locker.

She hissed, "I wouldn't go to a Spurs match with Craig if you paid me. You don't know me at all, do you?" Then she thrust an envelope in my hand before walking off. I ripped the envelope open. Inside were five one-pound coins and a note: "Here's the money I owe you. I HOPE YOU CAN BUY YOURSELF A NEW ATTITUDE WITH IT."

She'd pressed down so hard with her pen there were little tears on the paper. The words seemed to jump up and hit me in the face. I blinked furiously.

I'd over-reacted, hadn't I? Just because you think something, doesn't mean you're going to do it. In the heat of the moment you can think all sorts of wild things.

Cally had no intention of really giving Craig the Spurs ticket. I should have realized that. I'd acted foolishly. I'd acted without thinking. But these days I never seemed to have the time to hear my own thoughts. I was too busy listening in to everyone else.

I tried to patch things up with Cally. But every time she blanked me out. The following Monday I heard her talking about the Spurs versus Arsenal match. She'd gone with her cousin, Giles, who I knew she didn't even like much. I blocked up my ears and walked away.

Soon she and I got into the habit of

not talking. That wouldn't have mattered if I didn't miss her so much.

I especially hated walking home from school on my own. But I still had my trusty crystal. I went surfing: it was good fun tuning into complete strangers. Even if most of their thoughts were dull or made no sense.

One day, I thought, I'll do this and tune into something really bad.

And that's exactly what happened.

Chapter Eight
A Terrible Discovery

IT WAS FRIDAY afternoon. I was trailing home. I'd tuned into this woman who was singing to herself – a soul number which I'd never heard before – quite unaware that her song was flittering around in my head too.

But even that didn't cheer me up. All day long my head was full of voices and I had never felt so lonely.

Then I passed Cally's house. Cally had been away ill from school for the past two days. I stopped, hoping to catch a glimpse of her. Maybe we could talk more easily out of school. I wanted this silly feud between us to stop.

I didn't see Cally but I spotted Bess asleep in their porch. She saw me and started barking and wagging her tail. She was still my friend.

"All right, quiet now, Bess," I called. She heard me and obeyed right away. She was such a great dog.

Then I spotted this guy on the opposite side of the road. And I had the weirdest feeling that he was watching me. So I tilted the crystal towards him. He murmured in my ear: "The family's away tomorrow so I'll grab the dog tomorrow evening. Yes, it's very quiet round here, so it should be easy."

Then I had to let go of the crystal. By the time it had cooled down the man was already walking away. I had to follow him, discover more.

I ran up to the top of the road. There was no sign of him. He'd vanished without trace. Maybe his car had been parked close by.

I immediately jotted down a description of him: quite old, completely bald, grey suit and wearing glasses the size of a small television screen. Not the sort of person I'd imagine stealing dogs. But then I supposed dog-nappers came in all shapes and sizes.

Certainly there'd been a piece in the local paper about this gang who went around stealing dogs, then demanded a ransom for them.

A shiver ran up my spine. Was this about to happen to Bess? I had to do something. But what? My head was spinning.

I went home. Eating my meal in a kind of trance, I decided I had to warn Cally. I rang her up. To my surprise she answered. I immediately put the phone down. It seemed such a crazy thing to tell her. Hello, your dog is going to be stolen tomorrow. Don't ask me how I know. I just do.

Then I had a better idea. I'd send Cally an anonymous note.

I wrote:

BEWARE, AN ATTEMPT WILL BE MADE TO STEAL YOUR DOG, BESS, TOMORROW. DO NOT LET YOUR DOG OUT OF YOUR SIGHT. GOOD LUCK.

A WELL-WISHER.

I slipped out, popped the anonymous letter through her letter box and raced home again.

I'd just got in when the phone rang. It was Cally. She was not happy. "Did you send me this stupid note?"

"Me?" I quavered.

"It was you, wasn't it?" she said. "You tried to disguise your handwriting, but I recognized it right off. And it was you who rang me, then put the phone down again. I checked."

"Well, you see . . ." I began.

But Cally went on. "You're trying to get back at me with these stupid little pranks that aren't even funny. I mean, my mum's worked up enough with all this in the local paper about dog-nappers, without you making things up."

"I'm not making it up," I said. "I'm trying to warn you to keep an eye on Bess tomorrow."

"You know we're going away tomorrow."

"You are?"

"We're going to a wedding. I told you about that weeks ago."

She had, as it happens. But I'd

completely forgotten. "So what are you doing with Bess?" I asked.

"Miss West, our next-door neighbour, is looking after her. And she used to breed dogs, so she knows how to care for them."

I pictured Miss West in my head. She hadn't lived there long and the first time I saw her I thought she had purple hair. Actually her hair was blue, although that was nearly as odd – to me anyhow. But she was a nice woman, smiley and friendly. She was pretty old, though.

"Bess could be snatched quite easily from Miss West," I cried. "I reckon that's why they've picked tomorrow."

Cally sounded both puzzled and exasperated. "Why are you doing all this? Is it because I didn't give you my Spurs ticket?"

"No, no," I practically shouted. "I couldn't care less about the Spurs ticket. I'm just trying to warn you about something very serious. Honestly."

There was a slight pause.

"But how do you know all this?" asked Cally.

"I overheard some people talking in the road."

"What people?"

"Er . . . two people. Two men."

"And what did they say?"

A long breath. "They said, 'There's a dog in that house and we're going to steal it tomorrow night.'"

"Well, they don't sound very good

criminals if they discuss their plans in the road for everyone to hear. I don't think we've anything to fear from *them*."

There was no disguising the sarcasm in Cally's voice. "And tell me, did these two men carry a bag marked 'Swag' and did they –"

'Look, I wouldn't make up anything bad about Bess. You must know that," I interrupted. For one mad moment I wondered if I should tell Cally about the crystal. But there was no time. She'd already rung off.

I thought of ringing Cally back. But I didn't know how I could make my story sound more convincing. Then I wondered about calling her mum. She was a tense, nervous woman – in fact

Cally had told me, in strictest confidence, that her mum had been on tranquillizers for a while. What if, after speaking to me, she became so anxious she started taking tranquillizers again.

And maybe I'd misunderstood that bald-headed man. I'd only caught a snatch of his thoughts. And he really didn't look like someone who belonged to a gang of dog-snatchers.

I paced around my room. Then I heard the sound of laughter downstairs. I went down and discovered my parents and Alison, my sister, playing cards.

Alison is usually out with Tony, her boyfriend. But tonight she was staying in (although Tony didn't know that) as she didn't want Tony to take her for granted.

"Let him wonder where I am," she said. "Let him worry a little."

My sister's cracked.

But I joined in the game of cards just for something to do really. My dad was in one of his silly moods and kept trying to sneak glances at our cards. Of course I didn't need to look at the cards. I just set my crystal to work, then I'd "hear" them pondering about the cards they had and what they should do next.

I won every game.

"What's your secret, Matt?" asked Mum.

"I'm just a very skilful person, I suppose," I said. My sister made throwing-up noises.

"Well, let's have one last game," said Mum, "and see if we can dethrone the champion."

It was going really well until I came to my sister. I turned to her and then discovered she was thinking in French. I struggled to understand, concentrating hard.

"Can't understand my French, can you?" she murmured.

"It's your rotten accent," I began.

Then I stopped and gazed at her in horror.

She gave me a triumphant smile in return.

My heart started to thump furiously.

"Come on, you two," said Dad. "Stop looking at each other and get on with the game." I was so thrown by what had just happened that I lost the game.

"Seems like your luck has finally run out," Dad said to me.

My sister was waiting upstairs for me. "You're either an alien, which wouldn't surprise me," she said, "or you're using that crystal to read minds."

"What are you talking about?" I gasped.

"I watched you," she said. "Every time you fiddled with that crystal you picked up what cards we had. And then when I started thinking in French you knew, didn't you? You knew."

"Don't be silly," I said.

"I'm not being silly," she snapped.

"Yes you are."

"OK. Well, I'm going to tell Mum and Dad, tell everyone." She was yelling.

"Keep your voice down."

"Why should I?" She had this really crafty smile on her face now. In the end, the only way I could quieten her down was to let her "have a go" with my crystal.

"Let me see if I can pick up your thoughts." She held the crystal just as she had seen me do.

Then I had an idea. I'd seen a film once about these alien children who could read minds. Only, the doctor stopped them reading his thoughts by building this wall in his head.

I had to do that. Then Alison would believe my crystal couldn't do anything. And my secret would be safe.

I imagined a great, high brick wall. I pictured the wall growing higher and higher. No one could ever see over the top of it. It hid everything . . . everything.

Suddenly my sister let out a cry. "Ow, that crystal gets hot, doesn't it?"

"Yeah, it does that sometimes." Then as casually as I could, "Hear anything, did you?"

"Yes," she said.

My heart started to thump.

"I heard this strange noise like when you put a shell up to your ear."

This was the same noise I'd heard when I tried to tune into Bess. But she hadn't picked up anything else. And she seemed to lose interest in my crystal after that.

My plan had worked. Still, it had been a close shave. And all because I had to show off when I was playing cards.

I shook my head. Mrs Jameson kept the crystal's secret all her life. I nearly gave away its secret in three weeks – and to my sister, of all people.

I read Mrs Jameson's letter again. If only she'd finished it instead of putting those daft squiggles. I needed to hear her words of wisdom about the crystal. I had a feeling I hadn't used it very wisely.

I lay awake for ages thinking about Bess. I still wasn't sure what to do. I couldn't call the police, because where was my evidence? Maybe Miss West would let me look after Bess tomorrow. That was an idea. Then at least I'd know Bess was safe.

I finally fell asleep. Next morning I woke up with a start. I sensed something was wrong.

I reached out for my crystal. I always keep it on the little table by my bed.

But it wasn't there.

Chapter Nine
The Missing Sister

I SHOT UP in bed and searched frantically for the crystal. It was gone – stolen.

I knew who the chief suspect was.

I ran into my sister's bedroom. Normally she lolled in bed until midday on a Saturday. But not today. I tore downstairs.

"I don't believe it. Another one up early," said Dad.

"There'll be pigs flying past the window next," said Mum. They were both sitting at the kitchen table reading the papers.

I burst over to them. "Alison. Where did she go?"

"Into town I suppose," said Dad. "I told her a lot of the shops wouldn't even be open yet, but she just shot out of the door."

"You should have stopped her," I shouted, "because she's stolen my crystal."

Both Mum and Dad gave me shocked looks.

"Alison wouldn't do that," said Mum.

'She's done it," I replied.

"You go upstairs and search properly before you start making accusations like that," said Dad.

But I just knew Alison had my crystal. I thought I'd cleverly put her off the scent last night. She'd been the clever one pretending to believe me, then sneaking into my room and nicking my precious crystal.

What was she doing with it now – testing it out on someone? Or maybe she was about to sell it? I wouldn't put anything past my sister.

I raced into town after her. It was still early, only about half past nine. And there weren't many people about. I should find my sister easily.

She was often hanging about in the town centre by the fountain.

But today she wasn't.

I saw other people I knew and normally I would have chatted with them. But today I just rushed past. I saw everyone except my sister.

She'd vanished.

She must be somewhere.

Think. Think.

She might have gone to Tony's home. Maybe she was going to try the crystal out on him.

I sped round to Tony's house. He lived near Cally. And on the way I saw Miss West. She was taking Bess for a walk. Bess yelped excitedly when she saw me. But Miss West didn't look very sturdy at all. Anyone could steal

Bess away from her. She recognized me.

"I'll take Bess for a walk later if you want," I said.

'That's kind of you, dear," she said. "But to be honest, I enjoy the exercise."

"Well, er, actually I could look after her all day if you like." My mum wasn't keen on dogs but she couldn't mind just this once.

Miss West gave me a strange look. "I'm sure we'll be fine," she said firmly. I think I'd offended her. She walked away with her head raised in the air. I'll just have to keep coming back and checking on Bess.

Then I reached Tony's house. He opened the door. He gazed at me hopefully. "You've got a message from Alison?" he asked at once.

"No."

His face fell.

"But she was here this morning?" I asked.

"Oh yes."

"And was she holding a keyring – with a crystal?"

He looked surprised by the question. 'That's right. I'd never seen it before."

I smiled grimly. "And do you know where she is now?"

"I wish I did. We had this argument, you see . . . well, not exactly an argument. She came round here early, seemed very worked up, then started asking me if I loved her and how much did I love her."

Inside my head I made yucking noises.

"Then I was just answering her as calmly as I could when she went crazy and stormed off. I never said a word to her," he protested.

"No, but you probably thought something," I muttered.

"What?"

"Never mind."

"Will you tell her I'm sorry for whatever it is I've done?"

"I might," I replied. Then seeing his stricken face, "I will, though personally I think you're better off without her."

So I knew she'd called at Tony's and used the crystal. But where was she now?

Then suddenly it didn't matter any

more. For staring up at me was the crystal. It was sitting on the path right by Tony's bin. Alison must have been so angry she'd flung it in there. How lucky she was a terrible shot.

I was so pleased to have the crystal back. I clipped it back on my belt loop. I'd never take it off – and I'd put an alarm on it.

Then I became angry. My sister had no business nicking my crystal like that and then just chucking it away as if it were an empty crisp packet.

I arrived back home.

"Ah good, you found your crystal," said Mum. "Where had you put it?"

"I hadn't put it anywhere," I muttered, through clenched teeth. "Is Alison back?"

"Yes, she came home in a terrible state, really upset about something. But she's sleeping now and I don't want her to be disturbed." Mum gave me a fierce look. "I'm sure you can sort out your little misunderstanding later."

Little misunderstanding. Thanks to Alison I could have lost for ever my most precious possession.

I hovered in the doorway of Alison's bedroom. "Alison, are you awake?" I hissed.

No reply.

I wanted to wake her up but I knew Mum would go crazy if I did that. Instead, I stood glaring at Alison, holding the crystal in my hand. "I got my crystal back, no thanks to you," I whispered. "You shouldn't have taken it."

There was a slight pause, then I "overheard" Alison reply: "I thought you'd tricked me somehow. I wanted to see if it really did work."

I stared at her in amazement. Alison was still asleep. But not only was she able to hear me, I could pick up her thoughts too. Or the crystal could.

"I wanted to see if Tony truly loved me," she went on, then she gave a little sob.

I stared at my sister in disgust. Fancy wasting the crystal on something as pathetic as that. I didn't feel sorry for her at all.

"Then I got so upset I threw it in the bin," she said.

"I know," I replied. The crystal got hot then, and while I was waiting for it to cool down I had a brainwave. I wasn't sure if it would work but it was worth a try.

After I'd tuned into Alison again I said, "Repeat after me – Matt's crystal hasn't really got any special powers."

"Matt's crystal hasn't really got any special powers," she chanted.

This was weird, amazing. For the first time in her life my sister was doing what I said.

"I imagined the whole thing," I continued.

"I imagined the whole thing," repeated Alison, in a dull, expressionless voice.

"Matt, what are you doing?"

I sprang round to see my mum frowning at me. "I told you not to disturb your sister. Now you can come and help me in the garden. Come on."

I didn't have time to check if my plan had worked. But if it had — well, that would be amazing. I could not only read minds, I could control them.

I felt suddenly flooded with power, even though I was picking up weeds at the time.

I wanted to go back and check on Bess. But Mum kept me busy all afternoon, while my sister slept on. It was after six o'clock when I finally escaped. I sped off to Miss West's house.

It was lucky I hadn't been any later, for a familiar figure was ahead of me. It was the bald-headed man I'd "overheard" plotting to kidnap Bess.

And he was walking up Miss West's drive.

Chapter Ten
Trapped

I RACED DOWN the street.

"Miss West, look out," I yelled.

The bald-headed man turned round.
I thought he was going to say
something to me. But instead he
hurried on.

And Miss West hadn't closed her door properly. Slap-head could just walk into her house. And that is what he did.

This was getting worse and worse. Right now he could be tying up poor Miss West and stealing Bess.

I pounded up the drive, dizzy with fear. The door was still open. I ventured inside. "Miss West, it's me, Matt. Are you all right?"

The house was eerily silent. No sign of Miss West. Or Bess either. That was most unusual. Bess usually rushes to the front door at the slightest sound.

I didn't like this at all. I moved inside a little further.

"Miss West, are you –" I began. Then

from nowhere something hit the top of my head. I heard someone cry out. A woman's voice – was it Miss West? The next moment I found myself falling . . . falling . . .

When I opened my eyes the room still seemed to be spinning. Where was I? I was lying on a bed. I scrambled to my feet, then immediately sagged back again. I staggered to the window. I recognized Miss West's back garden. Cally's football had an annoying habit of landing there. I was upstairs in a bedroom. I stumbled to the door. It wouldn't open. It was locked from the outside.

I half ran to the window again. It was locked too – and double glazed.

I was trapped inside here. I

wondered where Miss West was now. I shivered.

In the garden Bess was lying on the grass. But Slap-head was coming over to her, waving this meat in his hand. I worked out it had to be laced with some kind of sleeping pill. As soon as Bess had eaten it he could carry her away.

Bess was edging nearer the meat now. I guess the smell was irresistible.

Thick hedges grew on either side of the garden. No one else could see what was going on. Only me.

I had to do something.

I rattled on the window. I called out. But the glass was thick and all Bess's interest was on the meat. She was sniffing it now.

In a moment I'd have to watch Bess fall to the ground and that man creep away with her. I'd probably never see Bess again. She could be sold to someone thousands of miles away.

My eyes blurred.

I twisted my crystal around in frustration. Inside my head I screamed, "Bess, that meat is bad. You mustn't eat it. Do you understand? It's bad."

I let go of the crystal. At the same moment Bess stopped and turned her head on one side. She always does that when she's puzzled. It was just as if she'd heard me. But that was impossible. I'd tested the crystal on Bess and hadn't picked up anything.

But, boil my brains, I hadn't thought of the other possibility. What if Bess could hear *my* thoughts? After all, dogs do hear many sounds which we can't.

I grabbed the crystal again and waited for it to become warm. The next few seconds lasted for ever.

Then I saw Bess pick up the poisoned meat. My heart stopped. She flopped down on the grass, all set for a good feed. I held the crystal even tighter. It must be warm enough now. Then I sent this urgent message to Bess: "Drop the meat. It's not good for you. Drop the meat."

Again she cocked her head to one side. She could hear me all right. But she wasn't very keen to obey me.

Cally and I were always telling her to drop things she found in the garden. She had a special fondness for forget-me-nots, even though they always made her sick. When she didn't want to drop something Bess would lower her head and grip whatever it was more tightly. She was doing it now.

"Bess, drop it! Drop it now." Inside my head I was shouting at the top of my voice. My lips started moving too — even though no sound came out of them.

All at once Bess did drop the meat and then she began wagging her tail as if to say, "Haven't I been a good girl."

Slap-head bent down beside her. I guessed he was talking to her, urging Bess to pick the meat up again.

The crystal had become scorching hot. My whole body screamed with the pain. But I daren't let go of it now.

"Well done, Bess, now run away from the man. Run away."

Bess obeyed this instruction at once. I don't think she cared much for Slap-head anyway. She started bounding about the garden.

"Good girl, keep running. Don't let him catch you," I urged.

We sometimes played "He" with Bess and it was a game she loved. Perhaps she thought she was playing it now as she went leaping through the flower beds.

Then she stopped and looked around her as if she was trying to work out where I was hiding. Slap-head didn't try and follow her. He just stared at her in bewilderment.

He must have thought Bess had

gone mad. He picked up the meat and began calling to her again. But she just hid behind the tree for a moment, then started racing all around the garden again.

The crystal slipped from my fingers. I couldn't hold it any longer. My hands were as red as raw beef and they felt as if they were covered in wasp stings.

But what did that matter? Bess was safe – for now anyhow. And actually my fingers seemed to recover remarkably quickly.

The doorbell rang. The ringing vibrated through the whole house. I sprang to the bedroom door and yelled, "Help! Help! Help!"

I've never shouted so loudly in my life. But in reply, just a deafening silence. They must have gone away, whoever they were. I banged on the door in frustration.

Suddenly I froze. I could hear another sound: a clicking noise. I recognized it too. It was the sound of Miss West's back gate. The next moment I saw Cally and her parents walking into the back garden.

I rubbed my eyes. I wasn't hallucinating, was I? Slap-head looked pretty amazed too. He dropped the meat and stood as still as a marble statue. Bess raced over to Cally and her parents, madly excited to see them. Then she began tearing around the garden again. She was determined to play "He" with someone today.

Slap-head was talking to Cally's

mum and dad. I wondered what lies he was telling them. But Cally's parents looked suspicious. I guessed they were asking where Miss West was.

Meanwhile I was pounding furiously at the window. Finally Cally looked up – and saw me.

Chapter Eleven
Another Shock

"It was just so lucky Bess didn't eat the meat," said Cally. "Do you suppose she knew it was poisoned?"

"I reckon she did." I patted her head. "She's a very good dog." I looked at Cally. "It was lucky you turned up when you did as well."

"Well, all day I was thinking about what you said and I didn't think you'd make that up, not about Bess. And then some of your other predictions have come true," said Cally. "So I pretended my tummy bug had come back. How do you feel now?"

"Oh, I'm fine," I said at once. It had been twenty minutes since I'd been let out of the bedroom and actually I still felt a bit shaky. Miss West had also been tied up and was very agitated. She sat drinking a cup of weak tea, while Cally's parents were interrogating Slap-head. They had already phoned the police.

He wasn't saying much, although I could see little purple veins pulsing on his head. In a low, dry voice he told how he'd just happened to spy Bess and thought he could get a good price for her. But somehow his story didn't seem quite right – not to me anyway.

"How did you know we would be away?" asked Cally's mum.

"I overheard you talking," he replied.

Then the police arrived. So Cally's parents and Slap-head left, while Cally and I stayed behind to comfort Miss West.

We sat chatting about what had happened and half by accident, I tuned into Miss West. I picked up something truly amazing. "This was such a mistake. I should never have let him talk me into this. Why do I always listen to my brother?"

Slap-head was her brother!

Did that mean Miss West was in on the plot too? Surely not, Miss West was nice – and she had a blue rinse, for goodness' sake. It was very hard to believe, or prove.

Then I had a brainwave. In the corner on the wall were some old black and white photographs. I got up and studied them carefully. Surely if Slap-head was her brother he'd be in one of these snaps. It took a while but I found one. He had a full head of hair then.

I nodded to Cally to come over. Looking a bit puzzled, she got up. I pointed at the photograph. "Who does that remind you of?"

Cally saw it at once. She rounded on

Miss West. "That man who was here, you know him. He's a relation of yours, isn't he? You're both in this together."

All the colour left Miss West's face. "My photographs," she whispered. "We never thought of that." Then she admitted Slap-head was indeed her brother.

"What were you going to do to Bess?" asked Cally. "Kidnap her and make us pay a ransom, or maybe you were going to kill her?"

"No, no," cried Miss West. "You mustn't believe that."

"I'd believe anything of you now," said Cally bitterly.

"You must let me tell you the truth," begged Miss West. The truth was this:

her brother was a dog breeder and he seemed all set to win a major prize with one of his dogs next month. He'd never won such an important prize before. There was only one obstacle: Bess. So the plan was to make it look as if Bess had been kidnapped when Miss West was looking after her.

"But honestly, truly," cried Miss West, "she'd have been safe with my brother's other dogs, and well looked after too. And as soon as the competition was over she'd have been returned to you, safe and very well."

"Thanks so much," murmured Cally with undisguised sarcasm. "Just for a stupid prize you'd inflict harm on an innocent dog, give me and my family a good deal of worry and hit Matt over the head."

"That wasn't meant to happen," said Miss West. Her shoulders sank lower and lower. "It's just when Matt turned up so suddenly, my brother over-reacted." She turned to me. "How did you know?"

"I saw your brother hanging around looking suspicious, that's all," I said. "And I got this bad feeling."

"Thank goodness you did," said Cally.

The phone rang. Miss West answered. "That was the police station," she said. "They want me to go too." She shook her head. I couldn't help feeling the tiniest bit sorry for her.

"Your mum and dad are on the way back," she said to Cally. "I'll just go and get ready."

"Shall we leave?" I asked Cally.

"No, I want to make sure she really goes to the police station," said Cally. She faced me. "If it hadn't been for you, poor Bess would have . . ." She shuddered. "Thank you, Matt."

I shrugged my shoulders. "All part of the service."

She went on, "I'd think you were a psychic person if it weren't for one thing."

"What's that?"

"How could you ever think I'd give my other Spurs ticket to Craig?"

"You would never believe me," I murmured.

"Well, you got some wrong information there," said Cally.

"You did go round Craig's house," I said suddenly.

"I was just being nosy," she replied. "But I didn't stay long. I always meant for you to have the other ticket, Matt. I was only teasing you. But it all went wrong. And, besides, you changed so much."

I looked at her curiously. "I did?"

"Oh yes. You never seemed to listen to me any more. You were always far away." Her voice rose. "It was horrible, it was like you'd been bewitched. You just weren't yourself."

"Well, I'm back now."

"About time," said Cally. Then she added, "The Spurs versus Arsenal match wasn't so great." A little smile crossed her face. "I think next Saturday's match will be much better."

Then I had to go to the doctor's for a check-up even though I said I felt fine.

Before I left, Miss West came downstairs to say goodbye. She apologized to both of us again. She even bent down and whispered, "Sorry" to Bess. She looked terrible; like a ghost.

She suddenly turned back to me and said, "That crystal you're wearing, Matthew. Excuse me for asking, but it reminds me so very much of a crystal a friend of mine wore. I always admired it so. Her name was Mrs Jameson."

That gave me a start.

"It is Mrs Jameson's," I said slowly. "She left it to me in her will."

"Well, fancy that. She and I worked together for nearly six years, you know. We were both secretaries, only she was much better than me. I could never read my shorthand back, she was always having to help me. It was such a shock when she left, and so suddenly too. Just marched out one day . . ."

It was then an idea sneaked into my head.

An amazing idea.

Chapter Twelve
Mind Reader Boy

I HAD TO wait until Monday before I could test it out.

I was bursting with impatience.

But after school I tore into the library. I stayed there until the library closed at six o'clock. I knew my mum would be cross but I couldn't move until I'd read every word of Mrs Jameson's message.

For at last I'd cracked the code and I'm sure you've guessed it as well. Mrs Jameson had ended her message to me in shorthand. Armed with a shorthand dictionary, I decoded: "Time is short and this is top secret but I know you will break my code easily."

I felt a real mouse-brain when I read that. The message continued: "I must tell you that my crystal has never brought me any happiness. I used it on the man I loved, my friends at work, and ended up a very sad, lonely woman. That is why I hesitate to give the crystal to you. Yet I know, if used wisely, it can be wonderful too. I think you are the one to discover its power for good. Goodbye.

Your friend,
Margaret Jameson.

P.S. There was only one person I never used the crystal on – and that was *you*, Matt."

I read her words over and over until I knew them by heart. Mrs Jameson's secret message to me.

She said the crystal lost her all her friends. Well, it nearly lost me my friendship with Cally. And my sister almost broke up with her boyfriend.

Did I tell you my sister apologized to me? Earth-shattering or what? It was after I got home on Saturday night. She told me she'd thought my crystal could read minds.

"But Matt's crystal hasn't really got any special powers, I'd imagined the whole thing." Her exact words. So I really had hypnotized her when she was asleep.

That should have made me feel very happy.

After all, I could hypnotize my sister again. She would have to obey my every thought. It sounded good at first. But I didn't want to turn anyone into my puppet, not even Alison. That would be seriously spooky.

So was Mrs Jameson's letter.

She was telling me the crystal had turned her into a kind of freak.

And the same could happen to me.

That's why I put the crystal away in my cupboard. And that's where it stayed for a whole ten minutes.

Then I saw Cally coming along the road with Bess. They were calling for me. Cally looked so happy. But if it hadn't been for my crystal . . . well, Bess would be far away now.

I took the crystal out of the cupboard again.

I decided I couldn't keep it hidden away. What a waste. But I'd make up some new rules.

Rule One: never use it on my family and friends.

Would you believe, I've kept that rule for one whole week.

Not that I haven't been tempted. You see, it's my birthday next month and

I'm mad keen to know what my mum's bought me.

My hand's certainly twitched a few times.

But I was strong.

From now on I'll only use my crystal for good things, like solving mysteries.

For with great power goes great responsibility – as Spiderman once said.

And what's good enough for Spiderman is good enough for Mind Reader Boy.

Don't worry, I'm not really going to call myself that. But if I can ever help you, remember there's no need to write or phone – just send a few thoughts my way.

I'll be listening.

MIND READER BLACKMAIL

Contents

Chapter One
Losing the Crystal

IT'S ME, MATT again. Up to a few weeks ago I was just an ordinary boy. Now I have a strange, eerie power. Maybe you've read about it, and how my whole life changed because of a crystal.

The crystal belonged to Mrs

Jameson, an old lady I came to know very well. She always wore this crystal round her neck. It fascinated me, perhaps because there were flashes of so many colours in it.

After she died Mrs Jameson left the crystal to me – with a mysterious note. She said no one else must ever discover just how special the crystal was: only me.

It took me a while to discover the crystal's secret, but what a secret. It can read minds.

How does it work? Let me give you a quick demo. Just say you walk past me and I want to know what you're thinking. All I do is move the crystal slightly in your direction, wait a few seconds for it to warm up, then I can hear your every thought, just as if you were whispering them right in my ear.

I can go on ear-wigging until the crystal gets too hot to hold. Then I let it cool down before I start again.

And it doesn't matter how far away you are from me. So you could be up one end of a field and I could be at the other. I can still listen in – or "tune in" as I call it – to you.

By the way, if you're sitting in your house you're still not safe from me. The crystal can eavesdrop through glass too, though not through walls.

Does this sound a bit weird, a bit spooky? I suppose it does. But it's also totally brilliant, isn't it?

I've made some great discoveries. But the crystal has also caused me a fair amount of hassle, especially with Cally, my best mate. After which I made a rule never to use the crystal on my family or good friends again.

I thought I'd learnt all I needed to know about my crystal. But I hadn't. And lately some incredible things have happened which I'd really like to tell you about.

It all started when I did something deeply shaming: I lost my crystal. How could I have been so careless? And with something so precious too. It happened the night of Craig's party. Some of you have met Craig before. If you haven't, I'll describe him to you in three words: sad, slimy, rich.

So why was I going to his party? Good question. But everyone else was going and I suppose I didn't want to miss out. Even though I knew it would depress me to see exactly how big Craig's house was and how much money was wasted on him.

Still, the party was OK-ish: lots of food anyhow. Craig, of course, was just bursting with smugness and spent the whole time showing off. So, actually, did his parents.

His mum was wearing these trendy leather pants and platform shoes. She even had an earring in her nose. I saw Cally staring at her and, just for a laugh, I broke my rule of not tuning in to friends. And Cally was thinking: "She's too old and wrinkly to be wearing an earring in her nose. She just looks ridiculous."

I turned to Cally. "Craig's mum is too old and wrinkly to be wearing an earring in her nose. She just looks ridiculous."

Cally gave a little gasp on hearing me repeat her thoughts but then she quickly said: "Oh, you're so cruel, Matt, she looks all right." I just grinned to myself.

Later we played "Murder in the Dark". Of course there were masses of places to hide. I hid under the stairs. I knew someone was nearby. I could hear him wheezing softly. It sounded exactly like Craig. I decided to check, and reached out for my crystal. I always keep it on my belt. Only it wasn't there.

Well, I was frantic. I forgot all about the game. I searched everywhere for it. Cally joined in too. Finally, she said: "Don't worry, I'll buy you another crystal when I get my birthday money."

How could I tell her the crystal was irreplaceable, priceless?

Craig pretended to hunt for it too. "I'm sure it will turn up, Spud." (That's my nickname because my nose looks a bit like a potato. Hardly anyone calls me that now, except Craig.) But I had the strangest feeling Craig knew more than he was letting on.

Craig doesn't really like me much. (He does like Cally, but that's another story.) So he'd enjoy hiding my crystal and then seeing me sweat as I searched everywhere for it.

Some of us were sleeping over. Cally was sharing a room with two other girls and I was sharing with a boy called Mark.

Mark fell asleep almost at once. The bedroom was very hot: Craig's family could obviously afford to leave the heating on all night. Normally I'd have drifted off to sleep too. But that night I tossed and turned. Where was my crystal?

I was more certain than ever that Craig knew where it was. His room was next to mine. Should I just barge in there and interrogate him?

Suddenly I heard a cry which made me shoot up in bed.

It was Craig – and he was calling for help.

Chapter Two
The Whispering Ghost

NORMALLY I WOULDN'T have lifted a fingernail to help Craig. But there was something about that cry. It sounded desperate. And I seemed to have been the only one who'd heard him. Mark was still sleeping peacefully.

I scrambled out of bed and crept next door.

Craig was standing right by the door. He made me jump. Then I was nearly sick. He was wearing disgusting bright red pyjamas which had his initials on the top pocket.

"What's the matter with you?" I asked.

He didn't answer. He looked as if he'd been turned to stone.

Something weird was going on here.

Then, for the first time, he seemed to notice me. He put his face right up to mine. It was covered in sweat. "I've just heard a ghost."

I'd have laughed except he looked so pale, and he was shaking.

"It was here in my bedroom," he went on. "I heard it whispering at me."

"Whispering," I repeated. Straight away I thought of my crystal. But how could it be mixed up in this? Unless Craig had fallen asleep holding it.

Then Craig's parents rushed in. They were both in their initialled bright red pyjamas too. The three of them looked as if they'd just escaped from the *Starship Enterprise*.

"We thought we heard you cry out," gushed his mum. They perched either side of him on the bed.

Craig told them about the ghostly whispering, while I prowled around his bedroom searching for my crystal. Then his parents, oozing concern, took Craig downstairs for "a sugary drink to calm him down".

I was convinced my crystal was in this room somewhere. I had to find it.

Then, out of nowhere, a voice whispered loudly: "I'm not going to hang around. That wind's got a real sting of winter in it."

It was like someone whispering through a loud-hailer at me. But the room was empty. I drew back the thick curtains. A man in a heavy dark coat was walking vigorously down the road. Was it his thoughts I'd just heard? But how? The crystal only worked when someone was holding it, didn't it?

I glanced down, and there was my crystal, wedged behind the radiator. My heart beat excitedly.

So Craig had found the crystal, just as I'd suspected, and hidden it behind his radiator. That was a really mean thing to do, even for him.

I bent down to grab it, then nearly dropped it again. The crystal was scorching hot. I touched the radiator. That was boiling too.

Suddenly, I had an idea. The crystal must have caught the heat from the radiator. Then as it got hotter it started picking up thoughts through the window. The hotter it got, the louder it got: beaming thoughts into Craig's bedroom in full stereosonic sound. No wonder he was so terrified.

I heard footsteps coming up the stairs. I was about to rush out with my crystal but then I decided to teach Craig a lesson. I nearly laughed out loud at my idea. Still, Craig deserved it.

I hastily returned the crystal to its place behind the radiator, exactly as I'd found it, tilted slightly towards the window.

I crept back to my room. I waited for Craig's parents to leave. They were ages. I heard them reassure Craig he wouldn't have any more bad dreams. I grinned to myself. That's what they thought. At last they returned to their own room.

I started to get dressed. Suddenly I stopped. I didn't need to go outside, did I? I could just . . .

I opened the window and stuck my head out as far as it would go. Would the crystal pick up my thoughts? I was about to find out. So was Craig.

But I was interrupted by a sleepy voice demanding: "What on earth are you doing?"

I turned round. "Hi, Mark, just getting a breath of fresh air."

"But it's the middle of the night – and it's freezing."

"Shan't be long. I'm just clearing my sinuses."

I pushed my head out again. Then I thought: "Tonight, Craig, you stole something, a crystal, which belongs to Matthew. That was very wrong of you. I am Matthew's guardian angel and I will send ghostly people to haunt you for ever unless you return it to its rightful owner. But hurry up, Craig, you haven't got long." For good measure I added, "Your parents can't save you this time . . . Beware . . . Beware."

"Haven't you finished yet?" Mark was sitting up in bed, staring at me.

"Yeah, my sinuses are completely fine now, thanks."

I closed the window. I'd just got back into bed when I heard footsteps.

"Pretend to be asleep," I hissed at Mark.

"What's going on now?" he muttered, but he did as I'd asked.

The bedroom door opened. It was Craig. He crept towards me. I heard a tiny chink as he placed something on the little cabinet by my bed.

I half-opened my eyes. It was my crystal. Its colours shone in the darkness. Craig tiptoed out again, closing the bedroom door quietly behind him.

Mark asked: "What did Craig just do?"

"I think he found my crystal for me."

"Funny time to bring it back."

"Craig's a funny guy. Still, better late than never. 'Night."

I looked down at the crystal nestling in my hand. I was determined I'd never lose it again.

Chapter Three
In Trouble

THE FOLLOWING NIGHT when everyone in my house was asleep I wrote up what had happened. I have a special exercise book, entitled THE THIRD EAR (the code-name for the crystal).

This is what I wrote.

AMAZING DISCOVERY: The third ear works when put behind a radiator and allowed to get hot. As it gets hotter the whispering becomes much louder.

IMPORTANT: When you hold the third ear only you can pick up the thoughts. But if it is behind a boiling hot radiator, anyone in the room can "overhear" what is being thought.

More soon.

I was so excited about all this I did something stupid.

My family don't usually keep the heating on at night. But we were having such a cold snap, my mum decided this once she would leave it on. So I couldn't resist jamming my crystal at the back of the radiator and then waiting to overhear the thoughts of whoever walked past my window.

Only no one at all walked past, and so I fell asleep. Later I jumped awake. At first I thought someone was in my room. In a way someone was. This man was hissing away in the darkness about why he hated his cousin.

To be honest, he scared me out of my wits. And the voice was so loud. I didn't like it at all. I must move the crystal right now. But then a shadow stepped towards me, and became my mum.

"Matthew, what are you doing letting your radio blare out like that?"

Of course, what my mum had heard wasn't anything to do with the radio.

"Sorry, Mum, I just couldn't sleep."

"Do you know what time it is? I've got such a lot to do tomorrow, with your dad away, and all."

"I won't switch it on again, Mum."

She huffed a bit more and turned to go. Then, to my complete horror, a voice hissed: "I'm sick of her going on at me for nothing. She's a real pain these days."

Mum was back in my room in an instant, glaring furiously at me. "What did you just say? How dare you be so rude, Matthew. And I didn't have a go at you about nothing."

"I know. Sorry. It was just a joke."

"A joke?" spluttered my mum.

I was terrified the crystal was going to pick up another passer-by's thoughts: maybe a woman this time. How could I explain that?

Desperate to get rid of Mum, I buried myself down in my bed. "Sorry again, Mum. 'Night," I burbled.

And I tell you, the very second she left I was out of bed, yanking my crystal away from the radiator. Only it was so hot I dropped it on the carpet. I had to scoop it up in a tissue and then leave it on the little table by my bed. I was very angry with myself. I'd been a real banana-brain tonight.

Next morning at breakfast the atmosphere was distinctly chilly. This was a shame, as lately Mum and I had been getting on well. And I was mad keen to have a dog. Mum wasn't. But I'd started to talk her round, and only last night she and I had chatted about adopting a dog from the local Animal Rescue Centre. Some chance now.

At school the first person I saw was Craig, which really cheered me up! I kept noticing him giving me these sly glances. It was as if he were studying me. I became uneasy. Had Craig guessed there was something special about my crystal? Surely not.

Then something happened which wiped all that from my mind. It was Cally's birthday in a couple of weeks. I was planning to get her something to do with Spurs (she is their number one fan). But I wasn't sure what, as she had so much supporters' stuff already. Anyway, I was waiting for her after school. We always wait for each other by the lockers. She came rushing over to me. "Oh my gosh," she said. "You'll never guess what's happened."

"Amaze me."

"Craig's just given me this for an early birthday present." She waved her left hand at me. On it now were two watches: her old one, and a brand new, big, chunky diver's watch, complete with stop-watch button and an alarm. I could hardly bear to look at it.

"That must have cost a few quid," I muttered.

"I wasn't expecting it at all."

"It's a wicked waste of money."

She nodded.

"And I mean, there are some things you just don't do."

"I was really shocked."

"But you're still going to wear it?"

"Well, yes." Her voice fell. "I do need a new watch, and anyway, I don't think he can take it back."

I didn't say much else. I was too

eaten up with jealousy and anger. I could never compete with a present like that. Trust Craig to throw his money about. And I knew why he was throwing his money about too. He wanted to go out with Cally.

We'd always been rivals where she was concerned. Cally and I had been best friends for hundreds of years – well, two, to be precise. For a while now I'd wondered if she and I would one day go out together. I wanted that very badly. But I wasn't sure if . . . well, to be honest, I wasn't sure if Cally liked me enough.

That's what stopped me asking her out. But I couldn't afford to dither any more.

I had to find out.

Or, rather, my crystal would.

Chapter Four
Helping Cally

ON FRIDAY, AFTER school, I decided to discover – with the help of my crystal – what my chances with Cally were.

There was only one place private enough for this. The oak tree in a wood just a stone's throw away from Cally's house.

Cally and I love tree-climbing. But the oak tree was our favourite because it was quite easy to climb: there was even a hole in the trunk where you could lift yourself up. And, best of all, about halfway up, it had a wide comfortable branch that was just right for sitting on. So in the summer Cally and I would sit there for hours, telling spooky stories and talking about things. There was also an epic view, stretching right across our village and the town beyond.

But now it was the beginning of October and Cally looked stunned when I suggested climbing our oak tree.

"Be a bit cold, won't it?" she said.

"We've got coats on."

She smiled. "Oh, why not?"

Climbing up a tree in a coat and scarf is actually quite hard. Our sleeves kept catching on the branches, so we were stopping all the time to disentangle ourselves.

"This is a bit like swimming with your clothes on," cried Cally.

"Can't say I've ever tried that," I replied.

We picked our way to the branch, settled ourselves, then Cally said: "So, what do you want to talk about?"

"Well, nothing really."

"Yes you do. Come on – and hurry up. It's freezing."

Well, I knew I couldn't ask her outright if she liked me. I had to build up to it. So I said: "I just wanted to chat about the cinema."

"The cinema," she echoed.

"Yeah. I just wondered what actors you like these days," I said, with my crystal poised ready.

Now, I know what you're thinking – I'd forgotten my vow not to use the crystal on Cally. Well, I hadn't forgotten my vow, exactly. I'd just decided if the crystal found out she didn't fancy me I'd be saving Cally loads of embarrassment too.

So Cally rattled on about what movie stars she liked. While the crystal heard: "I've got a horrible feeling I know why Matt is asking me these questions. I really hope I'm wrong."

That didn't sound very promising. But I pressed on. "Do you prefer guys with blond hair or dark hair?" (I've got black hair.)

She gabbled something about how

"it depended on the rest of the guy's face". But I was too busy listening to my crystal: "I'm going to pretend I don't know what this is leading up to. But I do. I've always dreaded this moment. Matt's going to ask me out, isn't he?"

There wasn't much point in asking any more questions. I knew the outcome: no sale.

But then I "overheard": "Of course I do think Matt is fit." Immediately a great big smile plastered itself across my face.

"What are you smiling at?" asked Cally.

"Nothing." I started to giggle. Cally thinks I'm fit.

"Come on, tell me," said Cally.

"No, I just feel good, that's all," I said.

But I couldn't get rid of that smile. "You were saying why you don't like boys with blond streaks."

She carried on talking, while the crystal "overheard": "Matt's behaving very oddly tonight. But he mustn't ask me out, because if we go out together and then break up . . . why, we'll end up nowhere. And I'll have lost my best friend. I can't risk that. Besides, tonight couldn't be a worse time . . . not when I'm so worried and upset. I'm surprised Matt hasn't noticed."

"You're worried about something, aren't you, Cally?" I asked.

She started. And for the first time I noticed how pale and washed-out she looked.

"If anyone realized, I knew it would be you," she said. "There's just a terrible atmosphere in my house at the moment." She stared out at the thousands of roofs and aerials below us. "My parents are really upset about something. They keep whispering in corners. Either they're about to get divorced or it's to do with me. I know they're cross about all my low marks at school. So I wouldn't be surprised if they're plotting to send me away to another school."

I sat up. "They mustn't do that."

"I just wish they'd tell me what's wrong. But they won't and it's really doing my head in."

"I'm not surprised."

Right then I decided I'd solve this mystery for Cally: me and my crystal. I felt a bit like those knights in old tales, who, before they can win the hand of the girl, have to perform a daring task.

I performed my daring task on Saturday afternoon. I was sitting inside the kitchen with Cally and her pet dog, Bess. Her dad was out in the garden, vigorously brushing up some of the autumn leaves.

Cally was asking me about the history homework. She was anxious to do it right. I stood by the window, talking to her. But I had my crystal trained on Cally's dad. So it was like trying to listen to two different conversations at once.

Often people don't think in sentences, especially if they're very angry and upset. They just splutter out the odd word. That's exactly what happened with Cally's dad. So it took a while to work out what was bugging him.

But at last I'd sussed it. And I couldn't wait to tell Cally. So later that afternoon when we were taking Bess for a walk I blurted out, "I wonder if your dad's got worries at work. A lot of people do these days, you know. Maybe he's on a shortlist of six, four of whom will lose their jobs because of –" I repeated the word I'd overheard from Cally's dad – "restructuring."

"No, it's not that," said Cally. "My dad's job is totally secure."

"I wouldn't be so sure," I said.

We even had a little argument about it.

Then, the following afternoon, Cally rang and asked to meet up in the wood again. She sounded worked up. I got there early. But Cally was already waiting for me.

"Anything wrong?" I asked.

She smiled. "Let's go tree-climbing again."

It had rained earlier and the branches were wet and slimy and difficult to grip properly. We clambered to our spot.

Then Cally exclaimed: "I can't believe it. You were exactly right. I asked my dad outright if he was worried about losing his job. He looked totally stunned. Then Mum came in and they both told me about this — and it was exactly the word you used — restructuring.

"Dad's certain he's for the chop. He said he and Mum hadn't told me as there was no sense in me worrying as well. If they'd only realized . . ." She smiled at me. "But what I don't get is how you knew. I mean, you were only in our house for about half an hour but you worked it all out."

"Just a lucky guess . . . I guess." I wanted to change the subject now.

"But it's uncanny. I mean, he's on a shortlist of six, and four of them will lose their jobs, exactly as you said."

I realized I'd given Cally too many details. I shifted uneasily. "Lucky guess," I repeated.

Cally wasn't convinced. I could tell. I went on: "And then it happened to this uncle of mine."

"What uncle?"

"Raymond, Uncle Raymond." That was the first name which came into my head.

"I've never heard you mention him."

"No, well, I don't tell you about all my relations. He's not very interesting anyhow. I don't see him much. I just know he was on a shortlist and lost his job."

"Where did he work?"

"Er, Birmingham. In this factory."

"Does he still work there?"

"Yes, he does."

"And you've visited him in Birmingham?" This was turning into an interrogation.

"Once or twice . . . long time ago now." Then I hastily changed the subject. We sat talking about much more important things: like how I could persuade my mum to get a dog.

Grey darkness was rising up like smoke now, blotting out our marvellous view. A sparrow came bombing towards the oak tree, discovered us roosting there, and started flapping like mad before it shot away again.

"Poor thing, discovering us in its house," said Cally.

I was about to reply when suddenly Cally started whispering. I thought for a moment I'd activated the crystal without realizing it. But her lips were moving.

She whispered, confidingly: "You haven't really got an Uncle Raymond in Birmingham, have you?"

She took me completely by surprise. "Yes I have. Well, sort of."

"Sort of." I could see her smiling at me.

"OK, I haven't."

"I can always tell when you're lying, you know."

"Can you?"

"Tell me the truth now. How did you know?"

I shrugged my shoulders. "OK, you tell me."

"All right." She smiled again. "You've made quite a few lucky guesses lately, haven't you?" She leant forward. "Ever since you got that crystal."

Chapter Five
Telling My Secret

THAT GAVE ME quite a shock, I can tell you. Without realizing it, Cally had stumbled on my secret. Of course she was saying it as a kind of joke.

"So can the crystal tell the future?" she asked.

"Maybe," I teased.

"There's something magical about it, isn't there?"

"Very definitely." I was still messing about but not completely. Ever since I'd found out how special my crystal was I'd longed to share the secret with someone, with Cally.

It's a bit like someone giving you a football. Yes, you can play with it on your own – do kick-ups and stuff. But only for so long. After a while you've got to have someone to kick the ball to, haven't you?

That was exactly how I felt about my crystal. It was only half the fun with just me knowing about it. And yes, I'll admit I wanted to impress Cally too.

Of course I remembered what Mrs Jameson had said: how I must keep the secret. But way up here, with Cally, I felt suddenly reckless, and daring.

"Do you really want to know how I found out about your dad?"

"Yes," she cried. The leaves were forming a pattern of shadows over her face. I could hardly see her. It made me feel as if I were talking to her in a dream.

"I've wanted to tell you for so long, Cally."

"Tell me what?" she screamed.

"Do you promise to keep what I tell you a secret?"

"I promise to throw you off this tree if you don't tell me right now."

"OK. I knew what was worrying your dad because I used my crystal to read his mind."

The wind stirred. It set the branches

rattling and shaking. Even the smallest breeze sounds much louder when you're up a tree.

Cally smiled at me. "So you can read minds?"

"With my crystal, I can read anyone's mind – even yours."

"Prove it."

"All right, I will. Think of a number and I'll tell you what number it is."

"Will you? Right, I'm thinking of my number."

"Wait a sec. You've got to let the crystal warm up."

"Oh, it has to warm up, does it? A bit like my nan's old telly."

She was laughing, while I frowned with concentration. "Now, think of your number."

And into my head she whispered:

"What is Matt up to now? He acts so funny sometimes."

"Think of your number," I urged.

The crystal picked up: "This is silly but seven . . . my number's seven."

I stared across at her. "Your number's seven."

A gasp escaped from her lips. But then she said: "Come on Matt, that's an old trick. People always think of seven, don't they?"

I shook my head.

"So how were you able to do that? You've got it out of a book, haven't you?"

I shook my head again.

"And stop shaking your head at me. This has got to be a trick. You can't really read minds with that crystal."

Suddenly the tree shook. The leaves

around us were going like the clappers now. It was almost as if the tree was trying to talk to me, warning me to stop, while Cally still wasn't convinced.

But I couldn't stop now. I held the crystal in my hand again. "Think of a word, any word you like, a word that doesn't exist if you like." I spoke really quickly, like an eager salesman. "Go on."

She gave an uneasy laugh, then half-closed her eyes. At once the word came through to me: "Spuckle."

"Spuckle." I grinned. "What kind of word is that?"

"I know." She smiled, but then her smile vanished into the darkness. "But how were you able to . . ." Her voice fell away. "How exactly did you do that?"

I waved the crystal at her.

"No, no."

And I "overheard": "If this is some kind of joke, Matt's carrying it too far."

"It's not some kind of joke, Cally," I said.

She choked off a cry. She drew back from me. Then, all at once she started to scramble down the tree.

"Cally, where are you going?"

"Why don't you wave your crystal at me and find out," she cried. "No, I'll save you the trouble. I'm getting as far away from you as possible."

Chapter Six
The Crystal's Powers

I WATCHED CALLY with mounting horror. I couldn't let her go like this. What a mess.

"Cally, come back." I started to clamber down after her. She was so worked up I was worried she might fall. But it was me who lost my footing.

The worst thing about falling from a tree is you drop down backwards. So you can't do it in a cool way or make out you meant to do it. And you look so completely undignified people can react in only one way: by laughing loudly.

That's what Cally did.

Suddenly I wasn't scary any more – just ridiculous.

I had to laugh too – until I realized that I had lost my crystal again. It must have slipped off my belt when I fell.

"The crystal's gone," I cried, struggling to my feet.

It was Cally who found it. It had rolled on to a pile of dead leaves.

"Here's your magic crystal," she said.

"Thanks." I carefully put it back on my belt.

She knelt down beside me. "So what am I thinking now?"

I tilted my crystal towards her, and moments later I "overheard": "It's incredible if it's true, but spooky too. The person with that crystal has got so much power."

Then I repeated word for word what she'd been thinking.

She stared at me. "I don't know what to say — or think. It's just incredible."

I nodded, enjoying her wonderment.

"So how long have you had the crystal?"

We went back up the tree and I told her the whole story. She listened, hardly saying anything, only exclaiming at certain events.

When I'd finished she said: "And you haven't told anyone else about your crystal's powers?"

"Only you."

"Only me." She let out a sigh. "Thanks, Matt, and I'm sorry if I . . ."

"Oh, come on, it's a bit of a shocker, isn't it?"

"And it will work on anyone?"

"Oh yes."

She grinned. "Prove it."

We climbed back down and made for the high street. There was hardly anyone about. The first person we saw — of all people — was Craig. He just nodded and waved at us. He was sitting on a wall by himself on the opposite side of the road. I let Cally borrow the crystal. She tapped into him. Afterwards I asked her what Craig had been thinking.

She smiled. "First of all he wondered if we'd noticed his new trainers."

"How pathetic."

"Then he couldn't understand why I was going around with you and not him. Bit sad really."

"Don't go feeling sorry for him," I cried accusingly.

"I'm not."

"The nerve of him thinking that," I muttered.

Next we spotted a well-dressed man with thinning brown hair strolling in front us. Again I let Cally tune into him. He was imagining himself scoring the winning goal at a cup final. Cally kept whispering bits to me.

Then she rushed forward, tapped the man on the shoulder and said: "Brilliant goal."

The man let out a cry and jumped right up in the air, just as if a firework had exploded in his trousers.

"Did you see that?" exclaimed Cally. "Look at him."

The man was now half-running away from us. He kept turning back, gazing at us in fear and amazement.

"He can't believe his ears," cried Cally.

"And are you surprised?" I replied. "You've just read his most private, secret thoughts. Actually, we've got to be careful."

"I know, I know." She shook her head. "This crystal is so incredibly powerful, isn't it?"

We were silent for a moment, then we thought of that man leaping up into the air and we both started to laugh. Soon, tears were falling down our faces and still we couldn't stop.

After that we climbed up the tree

again. It was getting late. We should have both set off home now. But neither of us could stop talking about the crystal.

Then Cally said: "On Friday when you asked me who I liked . . . you used the crystal on me, didn't you?"

I hung my head a little. "Afraid so."

"And you picked up that I thought you were fit?"

Immediately a smile started to form across my face.

"But I was afraid if we went out together it would ruin our friendship."

"Yes," I said quietly.

"Yet, tonight," she said, "you took a chance telling me about the crystal. I think I can take one too. So if you still want to go out with me . . ."

I could only nod.

Happiness took all my words away.

We agreed we wouldn't tell anyone about us yet. People like Craig would make stupid jokes. We'd wait and pick the right moment.

"Will you promise me just one thing?" said Cally. "You won't ever use the crystal on me, because I have horrible thoughts sometimes that aren't true and well . . . I'd never have a private moment."

"I promise," I cried. "And if you ever find out I have used it on you, you can have the crystal."

"What?" she gasped.

"No, I mean it, because then I'll have broken my promise to you and I won't be worthy of the crystal."

I glanced down at the wood below. It was very dark and still and full of shadows . . . and then I saw one of those shadows start to move. It seemed to rise up out of the darkness.

My flesh froze. I thought at first it was Mrs Jameson come to haunt me for breaking my promise, and not keeping the secret.

Then it moved again.

I hissed to Cally: "Someone's down there."

"Listening to us?" Her voice was suddenly hushed.

"Could be." I suddenly realized that we'd both been talking about the crystal at the top of our voices. Someone could be waiting down there, ready to jump us and steal the crystal.

We squinted into the darkness, then Cally cried out: "It's a cat."

Green eyes stared up at us, then

darted away. Cally let out a great sigh of relief. I didn't say anything but I still had a few niggling doubts. What if there had been someone else prowling about there as well as the cat? Someone crouching in the darkness, listening to everything we'd said?

But after a few minutes my doubts started to fade away. It had just been a cat, hadn't it? I noticed again Craig's watch on Cally's arm. And I said: "I wish I had a present to give you to remember tonight."

"Well, I'll tell you what," said Cally. "At my little cousin's tea-party yesterday I got this." She dug in her pocket and produced a gold-looking ring with a white sparkly stone. "I like it, so why don't you give me that?"

"A ring from a cracker?"

"It's the thought that counts." She handed me the ring. Then, feeling a bit silly, I gave the ring back to her. She placed it on her finger.

"One day soon I'll get you a much better one," I said.

"I'll keep this ring for ever," she replied.

I think she meant it.

Next morning I woke up feeling so happy. I was really pleased I'd told Cally about the crystal too. Somehow it had brought us closer together. And I was convinced that shadow I'd seen had only been a cat – until I reached my school.

There, sellotaped to my locker, was an envelope with my name in capitals on the outside. I ripped it open. Inside was a folded-up piece of paper torn from an exercise book. Printed in capitals was a message which chilled my whole body: I KNOW ABOUT THE CRYSTAL.

Chapter Seven
Blackmail

I SHOWED CALLY the note.

She looked horror-struck. "So you were right. Someone was eavesdropping on us."

I nodded gravely.

"Still," she said, "at least we know it was someone from this school."

"I bet I know exactly who wrote that note," I said. "It's got to be Craig."

Cally didn't look so sure.

"We saw him last night, didn't we? I bet he followed us." I frowned.

"Don't say anything yet," said Cally. "We don't want to rattle him, otherwise, well, he could do anything."

For the rest of the day I tailed Craig with my crystal. I didn't pick up anything incriminating at first. But then I "overheard" him thinking about the English test on *Julius Caesar* this Wednesday. He was worrying about it, as the results would go on our report.

Then, after school, a second envelope was stuck to my locker. I tore it open, feeling sick inside even before I'd read it. This one had been written on a computer. It said:

I will keep your secret about the crystal but on one condition. You must tell me what questions will be in the English test on *Julius Caesar* on Wednesday. Leave the questions in the empty locker (number sixty-six) on the bottom left hand side, straight after school tomorrow. Do not wait for me or try and see me.

If you do not follow my instructions I will tell everyone about your crystal. If you obey my instructions I won't bother you again.

I showed the note to Cally. She looked really miserable. "This is all my fault. If you hadn't told me about the crystal, none of this would have happened."

"Don't be silly." I didn't blame Cally at all but I did blame myself. And these mystery notes had taken the shine off last night.

On the way home we talked about what I should do.

"If I find out the questions I'll be giving in to blackmail, and Craig will come back again and again, won't he?"

"He said he wouldn't bother you again."

"Do you believe that?"

"Well, maybe."

I shook my head. "I could wait by the lockers after school and . . ."

"And what?"

"Fight him."

Cally started tut-tutting. "And what good will that do? He'll definitely go off and tell everyone about the crystal then."

Cally was right. I had no choice but to give in to blackmail.

Next day in English I looked around the class. I was pretty certain it was Craig, but I suppose everyone in the class was a suspect. I did a bit of surfing and picked up that other people in the class were worried about the test tomorrow. It didn't really get me any further.

At the end of the lesson everyone rushed off for lunch while I hovered around. Cally whispered, "Good luck," then she left too.

The English teacher, Mrs Stacey, had taught at my school for years. She was a good teacher: helpful, but brisk and no-nonsense. However, for some reason she liked me.

I moved towards her, clutching my crystal.

"Yes, Matt, what can I do for you?"

"I just wanted to ask you about the test tomorrow."

"What about it?"

"Well, I wondered if there'd be a question about the quarrel between Cassius and Brutus."

"Now, Matt, you know I can't tell you that. But you'll be fine tomorrow." She turned her back on me. "Now, off you go."

Mrs Stacey was thinking about a concert she'd be attending tonight, and how she'd do all her preparation in her free period after lunch.

This was dreadful. I wanted Mrs Stacey to be thinking about what was in the test – not her plans for tonight.

I uttered a kind of yelp.

She turned round, alarmed.

"What's wrong, Matt?"

"Nothing, Miss. I just feel a little faint. Is it all right if I sit down a minute?" I gave another little yelp and fell on to a chair.

I had all her attention now. She was leaning over me. I could smell her breath. It reeked of coffee. "Matt, do you want me to get Nurse?"

"No, no," I said hastily. "It's just I've been up late revising *Julius Caesar*."

She looked concerned. "But, Matt, you're a good student. You needn't worry."

"I do, though. I've been up worrying

for hours wondering if there'll be a question on omens and superstitions, or the battles at the end of the play . . ."

She pulled up a chair. She began to talk about *Julius Caesar*, and, more importantly, to think about it. The crystal picked up four of the six questions in tomorrow's test (and we only had to answer three). As I "heard" the questions I realized that I was cheating too. I'd know what was going to be in the test as well.

After I left Mrs Stacey I ran off to the back field and wrote the questions down. At the bottom I added: "I will not do this for you ever again."

Then at the end of school I made for locker sixty-six. It was dented right in the middle and the lock was permanently broken. Inside was a pair of old football boots. They smelt as if they'd been in there since the school was built.

I took them out and cleared the locker of all its antique sweet papers. Then I folded up the question sheet and slipped it inside.

Only Cally knew what I was doing. She gave my hand a squeeze. We walked out of school together.

"I've got to know who's sending me these notes," I said.

"But he said not to wait," cried Cally.

"I won't wait by the school," I said. "But I'll keep watch."

Our school was at the end of a road. Along the road was a bakery and coffee shop. Cally and I could stake out in there, then we'd see anyone returning to school.

"We must be clever," said Cally. "If we do see Craig or someone else from our class we've got to trail them, but they mustn't know we're on to them."

At that moment Craig passed the window. He was on his way back to school. We both ducked down.

"Did he see us?" asked Cally.

"I don't think so."

"Look, I'm going to trail him," I said.

"I think it's best I go after him," said Cally. "I won't get as worked up as you." She got up. "You wait here. I won't be long."

I ordered another coffee. But I couldn't drink it. My insides were turning somersaults.

And then I saw two more girls from my English class half-running towards the school.

I had a sudden, horrible thought: what if more than one person knew about my crystal? Maybe both those girls had written the note.

I had to follow them.

Chapter Eight
Breaking My Promise

THE TWO GIRLS walked quickly into school.

I followed at what I hoped was a safe distance. Craig was still my chief suspect, but anyone from my English group could have written that note.

The two girls were making for the

cloakroom. They walked over to the lockers. My heart was pumping away now.

"Here it is," cried one of the girls. She brought out a copy of *Julius Caesar*.

"Thank goodness I hadn't lost it," she exclaimed. "I knew I'd put it somewhere."

The two girls went off, giggling and chatting together.

A hand touched me on the shoulder. I whirled round.

"I thought I told you to stay in the café?" It was Cally.

"Did Craig take the note?"

"I'm not sure," said Cally. "He went past the lockers all right, but by the time I got near him he was striding off to the science block. I followed him there and saw him talking to one of the teachers about something. Then he went out of the school again."

I marched over to locker sixty-six. "We'll soon know what Craig's been up to."

I opened it up. It was empty.

"The questions have gone," I said softly.

Cally paled. "I'm so sorry, Matt. It's just I didn't want him to spot me, so I kept way back . . ."

"Don't worry, we've got all the evidence we need. It's him."

"We don't know for certain. And even if it was Craig, well, maybe he'll keep his promise."

Suddenly I had an odd feeling of unease. Did Cally know more than she was letting on? After all, Craig had given her that expensive watch. Was she trying to protect him? My fingers twitched around the crystal.

I'd promised Cally I'd never use it on her. But something wasn't right about all this.

We went through Ashton Wood. We were going to chat, up in the oak tree. But on the way, when Cally wasn't looking, I tuned the crystal on to her.

It was then I made a terrible discovery.

Chapter Nine
Message from Mrs Jameson

ONLY ONE THOUGHT was racing through Cally's mind: "If Matt finds out what I've done. If he sees the paper in my pocket . . . or somehow it falls out . . ."

I just looked at her. I was too shocked

to know how to react. Now she was thinking: "I must act calm. That's all I've got to do. Matt would never suspect me. This nightmare will be over soon."

She linked my arm. "Come on, cheer up. I think you might get a pleasant surprise. Craig's got what he wants. I bet he doesn't bother you again."

I gave her a thin smile. Her right pocket was the nearest to me. I pulled out a piece of paper. I recognized my messy handwriting right away. I felt sick. Cally's eyes were huge, while her jaw had dropped down almost to her throat.

"But how . . ." she gasped. Then she saw the crystal. It was still in my other hand. "You promised you'd never use it on me," she snapped.

"Never mind that," I cried. "You

wrote those notes, didn't you, Cally?"

Her mouth set sulkily. "Yes." Then she added quickly, urgently, "Matt, I had no choice. I was desperate to get some good marks. You know how my parents go on and on about my low grades. This was my chance . . ."

"So why didn't you ask me? I probably would have done it." I paused. "Yes, I would have done it – for you. But instead, you went about it in such a shabby way."

"It wasn't meant to be shabby. And I was only going to do it the once. I thought this was the best way. You must believe me."

"You expect me to believe anything you say now?" I paced about. "There I was, thinking how helpful you were following Craig for me. When all the time you were taking the questions for yourself."

"But what harm's been done?"

"What harm?"

Her voice rose shrilly. "Well, if you'd kept your promise to me you'd never have known, and we'd both be much happier now."

I turned away. I couldn't bear to talk to her any more. "I never knew you could stoop to anything so . . ."

"Well, now you do," cried Cally. "And can I have my questions back, please?"

I whirled round. We stared hard at each other.

"All right," I said softly. "You're only cheating yourself." I held the questions out to her.

She snatched them away from me.

She glared at me. "You said if ever you used the crystal on me you'd let me have it because you'd be unworthy of it. Remember?"

For a moment I thought she was going to try and grab my crystal. I immediately leapt back. She laughed mockingly. "Don't worry, I won't take your precious crystal."

She walked away.

I called after her. "Are you going to tell anyone else about . . . about it?"

She didn't answer.

I just stood there. Even in my coat I was shivering. Cally was the one person I trusted. It was the worst moment of my life. I'd never felt more lonely.

Finally, I crawled home.

I tried to revise *Julius Caesar*. But there were too many thoughts swirling around in my head. And every time I thought of Cally, a fresh storm of anger raged in my head. I kept blinking away tears.

Then my mum started fussing about me and being really nice. She hadn't been this nice to me since I had mumps, over two years ago.

Something was odd here. I used the crystal on Mum and eventually discovered that Mrs Stacey had called her, and told Mum she thought I was over-working.

I also picked up that Mum was changing her mind about getting me a dog. She decided I needed something to take my attention off my school-work. Normally I'd have been over the moon. But everything was ruined now.

Next day I dreaded seeing Cally at

school. It would just be so horrible. But in the end, she didn't turn up. She was away ill. So after all that fuss she missed the *Julius Caesar* test.

I only attempted the two questions I hadn't "overheard" yesterday. Every time I stopped and looked up, Mrs Stacey was smiling encouragingly at me. I felt such a fraud.

I kept thinking about Cally. I missed her. But I was still bitterly angry with her too. When she came back I wondered if we'd even be talking. Would she try to blackmail me again? I doubted that, but it was all such a mess.

What should I do now? There was no one I could go to and ask for help. How I wished Mrs Jameson was here now. She'd help me, for sure.

After school I found myself standing outside her house. There was a FOR SALE notice outside it, and the garden, which she'd looked after so carefully, was thick with weeds.

I didn't know what I was doing here. Mrs Jameson wasn't suddenly going to pop up and advise me. Not even the crystal could conjure up Mrs Jameson again.

But I held the crystal in my hand and thought: "Mrs Jameson, I can't believe you're far away from your beloved crystal, even now. I know I should never have told Cally about the crystal but I have done, and what should I do now? Help me, and advise me somehow, please."

Then I went into the local shop just across the road from Mrs Jameson's house. I'd been in there many times before on errands for her, and the old shopkeeper recognized me. We chatted for a bit.

I still had the crystal in my hand. Without me realizing it, the crystal was squeezing itself out of my hand. All at once it fell from my grasp and on to a stack of newspapers tied up with string, on the ground beside me.

I knelt down. It was our local paper. The crystal had landed on the bottom of the page. I picked it up. Underneath the crystal was a small photograph of a woman and a caption:

**LOTTERY WIN COST ME
ALL MY FRIENDS**
Full story page seven.

Without knowing why, I persuaded the shopkeeper to untie the papers so I could buy one. I walked home reading page seven.

This woman had won three million on the lottery. She said the news had changed her friends' attitude to her immediately. Their first thought was, "What's in it for me?" They all came to her with a shopping list of things they wanted.

She was indignant and hurt and felt her friends were just using her. She fell out with them all. But then she said: "I realized something as amazing as a lottery win was bound to set my friends dreaming. Now I want them to contact me . . ."

At home I read the article again and again. I kept thinking of Cally. If a lottery win set friends dreaming, so would a crystal which could read minds. Actually, my crystal was far more amazing than any lottery win.

I'd told Cally too fast, hadn't I? I should have built up to it over weeks. No wonder her head was turned and she did something which just wasn't like her. Really I was as much to blame as Cally.

I remembered suddenly how the crystal had seemed to just slip out of my hand, and land right on top of that particular newspaper, that particular caption. Had Mrs Jameson meant me to see it? Was that her way of advising me?

For a moment I forgot to breathe, I was so excited. I was certain it wasn't just a coincidence. I was certain of

something else, too. I had to sort things
out with Cally right now.

Chapter Ten
The Only Way

I WENT ROUND to Cally's house straight after tea. I felt really nervous. I still wasn't sure what I was going to say to her.

Her mum answered the door. "Oh, hello, Matt," she said. I stepped inside the narrow hallway. Normally she'd have told me to go right upstairs. Today she just gave me this embarrassed smile.

"How's Cally?" I asked.

"Well, she's had this terrible migraine all day."

"Could I see her?"

Cally's mum looked even more embarrassed. "Actually, Matt, she said if you called she didn't want to see you . . ."

"Oh, OK." My voice fell away.

"Have you two had a falling-out?"

"Yes, we have, actually."

"Well, I wouldn't worry too much. I think she's very stressed at the moment." She lowered her voice. "Last night I caught her tearing this piece of paper up into smaller and smaller pieces."

Immediately I wondered if she'd been tearing up the test questions on *Julius Caesar*.

"And her father and I want her to do well at school, but not at the expense of her health. Above all, we want her to be happy."

"Sure."

The phone rang.

"Oh, will you excuse me, Matt. I'm sorry, I can't . . . but I'm sure . . . well, you and Cally have been friends for such a long time, haven't you? Do you mind seeing yourself out?"

She rushed away. I thought for a second, then sprinted upstairs. Cally and I shouldn't be hiding from each other. We should clear the air right now.

I knocked on Cally's door. No answer. I opened the door slowly.

"Hi, Cally, it's me. How are you doing?" I tried to sound bright and cheerful.

Still no answer.

Then I saw why: Cally was fast asleep. I was about to creep out again, when I remembered something.

With the aid of my crystal I can talk to people when they're asleep. They hear me, and I can overhear their thoughts.

I held the crystal and, after it had warmed up, said: "Cally, can you hear me?"

"Yes, I can hear you." Her voice sounded heavy with sleep. "But how . . . Is this a dream?"

"Yes, Cally, you could say that."

"Well, I want you to go away. How can I make you do that?" she hissed.

"Look, Cally, listen," I began.

"No, you listen. I'm so ashamed about what I did to you. I should never have written those notes. You're right, it was very nasty of me. I don't know what got into me. And now I just want to curl up and die."

"But, Cally, it was my fault too."

"No," she whispered, "don't try and be nice to me. I can't stand it. I let you down. The crystal will always come between us now . . . Please get out of my dream. Leave me alone."

The crystal was scorching hot so I had to let go of it. Cally's words ran around in my head, especially "The crystal will always come between us".

It was that sentence which decided me. I knew what I had to do next.

Once, when my sister Alison was

asleep I'd used the crystal to hypnotize her. It was the only way to get her to forget about the crystal's powers. It had been for the best. Now I had to hypnotize Cally. I didn't want to. But I had no choice.

I picked up the crystal. It had cooled down enough. I said, "Cally, it's me again."

She groaned.

"I'm going to help you, both of us. Just repeat after me . . ."

Suddenly, I heard footsteps on the stairs. I had to act fast.

"Repeat after me: 'Sunday night never happened. It's gone from my memory.'"

"Sunday night never happened. It's gone from my memory," she repeated.

"And the crystal . . ." But I couldn't

say any more because Cally's mum was in the doorway, staring at me in bewilderment.

"Matthew, I told you . . ."

"I know, I'm sorry, but I thought I could talk her round – only she's asleep."

Then Cally muttered, "And the crystal."

Cally's mum leant forward. "What's that, love?"

"And the crystal," she muttered again.

Cally's mum just shook her head. "Poor girl, she's got herself so wound up. I think it's best you leave now, Matthew."

"Yes, sure. Sorry."

I ran down those stairs. If only I'd been able to have a few moments longer with Cally.

Now I didn't know if I'd wiped the crystal from Cally's mind or not.

Chapter Eleven
A Terrible Shock

NEXT DAY CALLY was still away from school. I wondered if I should go and see her again. But when I got home my mum was waiting for me, smiling. She'd arranged for me to choose a dog from the Animal Rescue Centre.

I was really excited. Dad was still

away, but Alison came with Mum and me. The dog was to be my responsibility. I could pick the one I wanted, only not a big dog.

The dogs were in pens and as soon as they saw us they started barking madly.

"How do you stand the noise?" Mum asked the assistant who was showing us round.

"What noise?" replied the assistant.

As we walked by the dogs they ran to the front of their pens, showing themselves off. All except one. A brown and white spaniel who hid in the corner of his pen.

The assistant pointed at the spaniel. "Poor Scampi, he was in such a bad way when he came in here, all his hair had gone."

"Oh, that's terrible," I cried.

"And he'd been so badly neglected he had to go on a special diet because his stomach had shrunk."

No wonder the dog looked so sad.

"He's very affectionate to us," said the assistant, "but he's still very shy, so he keeps getting overlooked."

"I think he might take quite a bit of looking after," said Mum, half-pulling me away. She was pointing at a terrier who was jumping about and wagging his tail furiously. "Now, he looks ideal," she said.

But my eyes kept going back to Scampi.

Suddenly I grabbed the crystal. I can't pick up a dog's thoughts from it, but dogs can pick up mine. I tilted it towards Scampi and thought: "Scampi, you're a good dog, aren't you? And do you want to come back with me?"

Scampi's ears pricked up. I knew he could hear me.

"Scampi, if you want to come away with me, go over to the front of the pen now. Come on, boy, hurry up."

The next moment Scampi was pressing his nose right through the front of the pen. I went over to him. He looked up at me, then licked one of my fingers.

I knew he was the dog I had to have. Mum sighed a lot but agreed. We had a special chat with the assistant, who said she would visit us soon to see how Scampi was settling down.

Scampi slept on my lap all the way home. "He seems to have taken to you, anyhow," said Mum.

When we got home Mum let Scampi

have a wander around downstairs. Then he just ran round and round the garden as if he couldn't believe his luck; he was somewhere decent at last.

Mum gave me a long lecture on how I was taking on special responsibilities with Scampi. He still had an infection in his eyes and needed eye drops twice a day. It was up to me to remember, not Mum. She also said how Scampi was never to be allowed upstairs.

"Couldn't he just put two paws in my bedroom?" I asked.

"If I see him upstairs, he goes back right away," said Mum. "He sleeps in the utility room, not on your bed." She made up a basket for Scampi, and said if he cried in the night, on no account was I to go downstairs to him, otherwise we'd never get any peace.

I wasn't asleep long when his whining woke me up. I crept out on to the landing. A floorboard creaked and Mum called out: "No, Matt, I told you, leave him."

But it was hard to leave him, especially as he sounded so unhappy.

Then I decided to try something. I stole out on to the landing again, held my crystal tightly and thought: "Scampi, can you hear me, can you?"

Scampi gave a kind of yelp in reply.

"Good boy, now listen. Don't cry, you're in your new home – and everything's going to be great now."

I went on like this for ages. Scampi's cries gradually became fainter, then they stopped altogether.

Next morning my mum congratulated me. "Well done, Matt, for not going downstairs to Scampi. I told you he'd soon settle down, didn't I?"

I smiled to myself.

The doorbell rang. I opened the door. To my great surprise it was Cally.

"Well, don't look so shocked. I've only been away a couple of days," said Cally. "And thanks for not coming round to see me," she added sarcastically. "That's why I've come to call for you. Are you all right?"

"I'm fine," I spluttered.

Then Scampi appeared behind my legs. Of course Cally loved Scampi instantly, and we were both playing with him until Mum shooed us off to school.

We walked along together, chatting about Scampi. Cally seemed very cheerful, her old self again. So had my plan worked? Had she forgotten all about the crystal?

"One good thing about being away," she said, "I missed the *Julius Caesar* test. Were the questions hard?"

I drew a deep breath. "Yeah, a real Mrs Stacey special. I could only do two of them."

"I bet I couldn't have done any of them. I always seem to revise the wrong things. Still, last night I had this long chat with my mum and dad, and they said as long as I try, that's all they ask. They were really nice about it, actually."

So far, so good. I was tempted to use my crystal just to check Cally had really forgotten all about its powers. But in the end I didn't. I'd promised not to use the crystal on Cally. And from now on I was sticking to that vow.

Then I noticed something. It gave me a jolt. Cally wasn't wearing the ring I'd given her to mark us going out together.

"Where's your ring gone?" I asked.

She grinned. "I was laughing about that ring with my mum this morning. I can't imagine why I've had that on my finger for the past few days. Mum thinks it's because I was over-stressed."

I stopped dead. "But I gave you that ring."

"Oh, very funny. I remember where it came from all right: out of a cracker at my cousin's party."

"But you gave me the ring to give to you because . . ."

She leant across and felt my forehead. "Matt, what are you gabbling about?

That ring is nothing to do with you. How could it be?"

She was smiling, but looking puzzled as well.

With mounting horror I realized what I'd done. I'd removed the crystal from her memory all right, but I'd wiped out everything else from that evening too: including us going out together.

I walked around school in a daze all day. How could I have made Cally forget something so important as us going out together? I'd just have to ask her out again.

After school Cally came back to my house. Mum had stocked up with doggy things, including a collar and lead for Scampi. We took Scampi for a walk, then introduced him to Cally's dog, Bess. She sniffed this new impostor suspiciously at first, but soon the two dogs were tearing around the garden together.

And there were celebrations at Cally's house too. Her dad had just rung through to say he hadn't been selected for redundancy. Cally's mum said she'd been going out of her mind waiting.

Then she took me aside and said: "I'm really pleased you and Cally have sorted yourselves out."

But we hadn't sorted ourselves out. That was the problem.

So later, when Cally and I were sitting in the garden, watching the two dogs playing together, I asked her out again.

She turned me down flat. She said:

"I've been dreading you asking me that. I do like you. Of course I do. But if we went out together, and it didn't work out . . . well, we'd have nothing. And I'd have lost my best mate. So I don't think I could ever take that chance."

I wanted to say to her: "But you did take that chance – just a few nights ago." But of course she didn't remember anything about that now. That moment was lost for ever.

Maybe she'd only agreed to go out with me on Sunday because I had a magic crystal.

I'd never know now.

That was the problem with the crystal. It mixed up everything, poisoned everything.

I was supposed to stay at Cally's for

my tea. But I said I felt a bit sick and would go home. Instead, I took Scampi for another walk. We ended up going further than I'd intended: right on to the outskirts of the town. Scampi was enjoying himself anyway, sniffing everything appreciatively.

But I felt as if I'd been punched in the stomach. I took the crystal off my belt. I stared into it, watching all the different colours twisting and curling like a nest of snakes.

"You ruined Mrs Jameson's life," I muttered. "And now you're ruining mine. What do I want to look into people's heads for anyway? It only makes you lose all your friends. You've brought so many bad vibes into my life, I reckon my life would be much better without you."

I threw my hand holding the crystal right back. I really meant to chuck it in the bin opposite me, you know.

And I probably would have done if a voice hadn't whispered right in my ear: "What am I going to do? Someone help me, please."

Chapter Twelve
Merlin to the Rescue

I FROZE. WHAT had the crystal picked up now? It would only mean more trouble. But it was as if I'd received a distress signal. I couldn't ignore it, especially as the voice had sounded so young.

The crystal was pointing towards a

back street I'd never noticed before. "Come on, Scampi," I said. "We'll have a quick look, then we'll go home."

A second-hand shop took up the whole street. Sprawled down one side were ancient armchairs, sofas and cabinets; opposite, in front of a huge garage, loomed a small army of clapped-out fridges and cookers.

A man lurked in the shop doorway. He was a large, sweaty-looking man with tiny eyes. Scampi gave a low growl.

"Tie your dog up before you come in here."

"Shan't bother," I replied.

It certainly wasn't him the crystal had "overheard". Scampi and I wandered on down the street. The man stood watching us for a bit, then he went back inside his shop.

No one else seemed to be about. Yet the crystal had definitely "overheard" someone. I held it in front of me as if it were a metal detector searching out buried treasure.

The crystal quickly found that voice again. This is what I overheard: "Mum said, get out of my sight, William, I never want to see you again. And she won't. But what am I going to do? I can't stay here." Yet the voice still seemed to be coming out of thin air.

We were at the end of the street now. All that faced us was a large brown wardrobe. Scampi gave another growl. "Do you hear someone too?" I whispered.

Suddenly I opened the wardrobe door. And there, shrinking at the back, was a small boy who couldn't have been more than five or six.

I stared at him.

He stared back at me.

"Any particular reason why you're sitting in that wardrobe?" I asked.

"Just leave me alone," hissed the boy.

"What's your name?" I asked.

"Can't tell you that."

"It wouldn't be William, would it?"

The boy jumped in amazement. "But how did you know that?"

"Oh, I know lots of things – like, you've run away from home, haven't you?"

"Yes," squeaked the boy. Then he added: "You're magic, aren't you?"

I grinned. "Just call me Merlin."

But the boy took me seriously. "You're not Merlin the magician?"

"That's right. Only I'm in disguise, so don't tell anyone."

"I won't," gasped the boy.

"Now, I command you to climb out of that wardrobe."

The boy obeyed me instantly. He was shaking a bit. I think he was worried I was about to turn him into a toad.

"Why don't you give Scampi a pat?" I said.

The boy knelt down and gently, cautiously, patted Scampi.

"Tell me, what are you doing here?" I asked the boy.

"Don't you know?" he demanded.

"Of course I do. But I want you to tell me."

"All right, Merlin. Well, you know I broke my mum's special vase. And I really didn't mean to do it, but now she hates me. She said I'm nothing but trouble and she's sick of me. She told me to get out of her sight. And so I did.

"She thinks I'm in my room, but I crept out of the house and this bus pulled up, and I got on it. I sat with this woman and two other boys. They asked for a half-fare to Jericho Road, and so did I. I used up all my money too.

"I got off with them, but they weren't very friendly. Then the woman said she was going to take me to the police station, but I ran and ran, and I've got to hide here . . . for ever."

"You can't do that, William. You'll have to go back," I said.

"I can't," he cried.

"I'm commanding you," I said.

"Oh." He looked up. "Will you magic us back?"

"No, we'll get the bus this time," I said. "I only use magic for special occasions these days."

The three of us caught the bus back to William's home in Clately. It was nearly seven miles away, and the fare used up all the money I had saved for Cally's birthday. William sat cuddling Scampi. He noticed my crystal and wanted to hold it.

"Maybe, later," I said.

Then the bus drew into William's road. Suddenly he pointed. There was a woman talking animatedly into a mobile phone.

"That's my mum," he cried, "and she's going to be so mad at me."

"No she won't," I said.

"Yes she will. She looks really angry."

The bus jolted to a stop. William hissed:

"I'm sorry, Merlin, but I can't get off this bus. Not even if you command me."

I thought quickly. "All right, William, I'm going to put a spell on you."

"Oooh." William looked both scared and excited.

"Here, hold my crystal."

He took the crystal.

Then I muttered (hoping no one else could hear me),

"Hocus Mucus, the magic spell will dawn
When this crystal starts to get warm."

A few seconds later William exclaimed: "It is getting hot, Merlin."

"Good, the spell is working. Move the crystal towards the window, and your mum."

"I don't want her to see me," said William, crouching down.

"Now, my magic spell is this: whatever your mum thinks will pour into your ear."

William looked at me, then let out a cry. "It's my mum talking right in my ear like you said. Can she hear me?"

I shook my head.

"She's saying, if anything's happened to William I'll never forgive myself. Never. All that fuss over a stupid vase. Now she's saying . . ."

The bus started to lurch forward. William looked at me, then screeched: "Make the bus stop, Merlin."

"Only you can do that," I said.

With that, William let out a great yell of "Stop" and the three of us scrambled off, just in time.

William's mum spotted William and came flying towards us at a speed any Olympic athlete would have envied. She and William hugged and kissed each other while Scampi and I felt a bit awkward.

But then William's mum insisted Scampi and I come inside for tea and cakes. We also met just about every one of the neighbours who'd all been out looking for William.

Then William's dad arrived – he'd rushed home from work. And later he insisted on driving us home (just as well, as I only had ten pence left) and telling my startled mum just what I'd done.

After he'd left, Mum said: "I'm really proud of you. If you hadn't discovered that boy goodness knows what would have happened to him . . . You know, you might even have saved his life."

Then she added: "Just one thing, why did William's dad keep calling you Merlin?"

"Oh, it's a long story, Mum," I said, and quickly changed the subject. Knowing I'd helped William gave me a good feeling. Of course it was the crystal, really. How could I ever have thought of chucking it away? That would have been so stupid – and cowardly.

Mrs Jameson must have realized I'd make some mistakes with the crystal. But she'd believed in me too. And one day I know I'll become the crystal master. Then, when I'm very old and have to decide who to pass the crystal on to next, I'll write down everything I've learnt. A kind of guide book.

Rule one will be: never use the crystal on your family, your mates – or your girlfriend.

No, Cally isn't my girlfriend yet. But I haven't given up hope. She did agree to go out with me once. It's just a shame she doesn't remember anything about it now. Still, I know she thinks I'm fit. And I can bask in that.

Whatever happens with Cally in the future, the crystal stays out of it. I'm only using my crystal on one friend at the moment. Can you guess who?

Well, I'll tell you. Every afternoon after I leave Cally I pick up my crystal and start beaming thoughts to Scampi. His hearing, by the way, is amazing. He can pick up from over a mile away.

I say to him: "Come on, Scampi,

come and meet me. Go to the door, there's a good boy."

At once he starts scratching at the front door, whining to be let out. Then he charges off and sits right outside the gate just as I'm about to turn into my road.

My neighbours think it's uncanny how he always knows exactly when I'm coming home. So, if I'm late because of football practice, Scampi will just ask to be let out later too.

He never gets it wrong.

Half of my road come out to observe this amazing phenomenon now. "It's magic to watch," one of them said yesterday.

Thanks to the crystal my life is full of magic. Just about anything could happen. Maybe one day I'll even pick up your thoughts. Wouldn't that be great?

I'll be listening.

Read more in Puffin

For complete information about books available from Puffin – and Penguin – and how to order them, contact us at the appropriate address below. Please note that for copyright reasons the selection of books varies from country to country.

www.puffin.co.uk

In the United Kingdom: Please write to Dept EP, Penguin Books Ltd, Bath Road, Harmondsworth, West Drayton, Middlesex UB7 ODA

In the United States: Please write to Penguin Putnam Inc., P.O. Box 12289, Dept B, Newark, New Jersey 07101–5289 or call 1–800–788–6262

In Canada: Please write to Penguin Books Canada Ltd, 10 Alcorn Avenue, Suite 300, Toronto, Ontario M4V 3B2

In Australia: Please write to Penguin Books Australia Ltd, P.O. Box 257, Ringwood, Victoria 3134

In New Zealand: Please write to Penguin Books (NZ) Ltd, Private Bag 102902, North Shore Mail Centre, Auckland 10

In India: Please write to Penguin Books India Pvt Ltd, 11 Panscheel Shopping Centre, Panscheel Park, New Delhi 110 017

In the Netherlands: Please write to Penguin Books Netherlands bv, Postbus 3507, NL–1001 AH Amsterdam

In Germany: Please write to Penguin Books Deutschland GmbH, Metzlerstrasse 26, 60594 Frankfurt am Main

In Spain: Please write to Penguin Books S. A., Bravo Murillo 19, 1° B, 28015 Madrid

In Italy: Please write to Penguin Italia s.r.l., Via Felice Casati 20, I–20124 Milano

In France: Please write to Penguin France S. A., 17 rue Lejeune, F–31000 Toulouse

In Japan: Please write to Penguin Books Japan, Ishikiribashi Building, 2–5–4, Suido, Bunkyo-ku, Tokyo 112

In South Africa: Please write to Longman Penguin Southern Africa (Pty) Ltd, Private Bag X08, Bertsham 2013